YELLOWSTONE HOMECOMING

YELLOWSTONE ROMANCE SERIES

PEGGY L HENDERSON

ISBN: 9781096694212

CHAPTER ONE

Madison Valley on the Yellowstone Plateau, Summer, 1838

"Matthew's dead."

Zach Osborne uttered the words that he hadn't been able to voice in nearly six weeks. Words he'd refused to believe. Something about saying them out loud made it real. Final.

His jaw tightened, every muscle in his body taut. Rage and anger surged through him, along with a pain so great, he wanted to shout into the wind at the injustice of it. He'd already blamed himself countless times for his brother's untimely death. He'd sworn revenge on those responsible. He'd cursed himself, the men who'd killed Matthew, and even his brother, for letting them get the better of him.

Zach mentally shook his head. He could place blame on everyone, but it wouldn't change the fact that his brother was gone. Shouldn't he be feeling different? Feeling something other than anger that Matthew was dead, yet he had survived? Matthew was his twin brother. They'd shared a bond that was unbreakable. They had a connection, knew everything about each other to the point of finishing each other's thoughts. Shouldn't he feel dead, too?

You do feel dead. A part of you is gone.

The worst of it was, he'd spent the last month dreading his homecoming to the Madison Valley. Dreaded what he had to tell his mother and father. The awful moment had arrived.

Zach focused his eyes on his mother, who stood directly in front of him. Reluctantly, he looked down at her. While she was petite and short, and the top of her head barely reached his shoulders, Aimee Osborne was a force to be reckoned with. Right now, she stared back at him, incomprehension and confusion in her eyes. He darted a quick look toward his father. Of equal stature, he could face Daniel Osborne squarely and look him in the eye.

"What?"

Zach's attention returned to his mother. Her feeble question tore at his already strained heart. She reached out and grabbed his arm, while his father reached for hers.

Zach swallowed. He couldn't bear to look at the pain and panic in her eyes. His usually composed mother, always strong in any situation, looked as if she was about to crumble to the ground.

"Matthew . . ." Zach's voice faltered, and he ran a shaky hand across his jaw, the heavy whiskers of his unshaven face scraping against his fingers. He swallowed, and cleared his throat. He sucked in a long breath, and tried again. "Matthew's gone, Mama."

He reached for her, and she fell against him. Holding the small woman in his embrace, the woman he'd looked up to all his life, even if he'd had to look down at her since he'd been ten years old, tore him to pieces. She trembled in his arms, then pulled back and tilted her head to stare up at him. Moisture pooled in her blue eyes. His father came up beside him, and Zach broke eye contact with her. Pain such as he'd never seen before clouded his father's dark gaze.

"Pawnee," Zach said quietly. His father would understand this single word. "Along the Platte," he continued, even though further elaboration was unnecessary. "Nearly six weeks ago, after we crossed the Missouri."

Stoically, his father nodded. He reached for his wife. Zach released his mother. Daniel enfolded her in his arms as if he could shield her from the pain of losing her son, and she sobbed against his chest. Zach cursed under his breath, and his vision blurred.

"Zach, you're home," a female voice called happily from somewhere in the distance.

Zach ran a trembling hand across his face, and turned to face his sister. He couldn't even force a smile. His sister, Sarah, rushed along the well-worn path that led from the cabin she shared with her husband to their folks' cabin. She beamed a bright smile, and threw her arms around his neck. Zach embraced her, and inhaled deeply. In a second, he would have to repeat what he'd already told his folks.

Sarah pulled out of his embrace. She looked so grown

up, no longer the little sister who'd always tried to prove to her three brothers that she was capable of anything that they could do, and do it better. Although she still wore britches and kept her dark hair in a long braid down her back, she'd certainly matured in the few years since her marriage to the most unlikely man she could have chosen.

Even though his brother-in-law, Chase Russell, had been a greenhorn several years ago when he came to this wild and remote land where Zach had grown up with his two brothers and sister, the man sure had learned fast. More important, he was a good husband to Sarah. He'd quickly become like a third brother to him. Zach's chest tightened. No one could replace the one brother he'd lost.

Sarah's smile faltered. Her forehead drew together, forming creases, and she cocked her head to study him. She glanced toward her parents, then scrutinized him with her blue eyes.

"What's wrong?" she asked. She looked around some more. "Where's Matthew? Don't tell me he decided to stay in Boston?"

A screech like the sound of an owl tore through the air, and Sarah wheeled around. A tiny person with long blond hair waddled toward them from Sarah's cabin, followed closely by a tall man holding another blond-haired child in his arms.

Zach shot a quick glance toward his folks. His father still held tightly to his mother. He gazed in the direction of the blond man heading their way. Chase was several inches taller than everyone else, lean, and looked every bit the confident woodsman. He reached them just as the little girl grabbed onto her mother's leg.

Zach stared down at his niece, Emily. He'd only seen her once, right after her birth two years ago, before he and Matthew had gone east to begin their studies at Harvard University in Boston. The other little girl in Chase's arms had to be his newest niece, Kara. Although she was already a year old, he and Matthew had only found out about her just before leaving Boston several months ago. They had joked about Chase being blessed, or cursed, with two daughters already in less than three years of marriage.

Chase beamed a bright smile, and held out his hand for Zach to shake, the little girl balanced easily on his other arm. Her face was covered in something white and sticky-looking, and her left thumb was firmly buried in her mouth.

"Good to see you, Zach. All done with law school? Where's the newest doctor in the family?"

Zach didn't respond. Chase's grin faded, and he glanced at their parents, then at Sarah.

"Why don't we all go inside?"

Zach startled at his father's deep and solemn voice. Although spoken quietly, the words held a commanding edge. He led his wife into their cabin, and Zach followed. He caught the puzzled looks Sarah and Chase exchanged. Sarah gathered Emily into her arms, and walked ahead of her husband.

"Where's Sam?" Zach asked, when everyone had filed into the main room of his childhood home. The less often he had to repeat his tale, the better. If his younger brother wasn't here, it would only mean he'd have to share his tragic news a third time.

"He's off hunting with Touch the Cloud. Unlike you

and Matthew, he prefers to spend his time in the woods rather than sticking his nose in a book or living in the city. He won't be home for several days."

Zach shot Chase a dry look. He fisted his hand at his side, ready to punch his brother-in-law and wipe that smirk off his face. Chase was a good man, but his constant baiting and teasing could get on a man's nerves. The pent-up emotions inside Zach were ready to explode.

"What's the matter, Mama?" Sarah asked softly, moving toward their mother, who was still wrapped tightly in their father's arms.

Sarah glanced his way. Zach swallowed. He looked at each of them again. His body tingled, feeling hollow. If he could, he'd melt into the floorboards rather than say the words again that made Matthew's passing final.

"Matthew and I ran into some trouble on our way here," he said, meeting his sister's eyes. "We were attacked by a group of Pawnee, and while I . . ." Zach's voice faltered. He cursed, and slammed his fist on the table.

Sarah gasped. Chase swore out loud. Zach raised his head, the people in front of him – his family – staring back at him expectantly. Four pairs of eyes filled with pain and trepidation.

"I watched Matthew get hit by an arrow while I was busy fending off a bunch of warriors. That's the last I saw of him. There were too many, and they took me prisoner. When I escaped a few days later, I tried to find him, but couldn't."

Zach sank into a chair. He raked his fingers through his hair. Why the hell had he survived? He couldn't even give his brother a proper burial. He'd searched for days before finally giving up hope that he'd find Matthew's body. The Pawnee, no doubt, had torn him to pieces and scattered his remains. Zach had been nearly starved, beaten, and weak, but he hadn't stopped looking.

"A family of Lakota took me in until I regained my strength. By then, it was too late to find any remains." Zach stared up at his father. "I tried to find him. I tried, but . . ."

His father reached out and placed a hand on his shoulder. "We know. Don't place blame on yourself. You would have died along with your brother."

Zach's jaw clenched. He leaped from his chair, renewed rage engulfing him. "I should have died with him. He was my brother, dammit, and I failed him."

His mother rushed to him, and reached up, clasping his face between her hands. "I lost one son. I couldn't bear it to lose another," she whispered. "You did nothing wrong, Zach." Her voice was hollow.

"How do you know he's dead?" Chase's words sounded far away. "If you didn't find a body, maybe he got away." He shot hasty looks around the room. "I'll go find Sam, and we'll organize a search."

Zach's scornful laughter filled the room. "It's at least a four-week trek to where the attack occurred, even if we push hard. I couldn't find him then. You'll never find him after all this time."

"It's worth a shot," Chase argued. "Where exactly were you and what were you doing when those Pawnee attacked?"

CHAPTER TWO

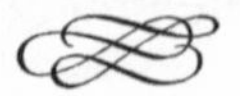

Six weeks earlier . . .

"Do you plan to get better acquainted with Miss Halsey when we get back to Boston?"

Matthew frowned at the question. He shifted in the saddle, and nudged his horse into a faster walk. Zach's lips twitched in the corners, casting a sideways glance at him. "I know you've seen quite a bit of her in the last few months."

Matthew continued to look straight ahead, his eyes trained on the swirl of dust in the distance. The endless grassland and flat, open prairie sent uneasy tingles down his spine. Time couldn't pass fast enough before he and Zach were home in the mountains. Even after two years in Boston, the wild land and its wonders that no one seemed to believe existed or took seriously, called to him. Two years was a long time to be away from the place where he'd grown up and called home for the better part of his life. He'd chosen to move east several years ago, but it sure felt nice to come home for a visit.

"I don't have an interest in Miss Halsey," he grumbled. "She's the one who seems to have latched on to me. The last time we spoke just before you and I left Boston, I told her she might have better luck pursuing you."

Matthew shot a quick look at his brother to gauge his reaction. Zach grinned.

"She's a fine looking lady, but I've got my eyes set on Bethany Milner. Once I've worked in Mr. Lanstrom's law practice for a while, I plan to court her."

Matthew grunted. His eyes continued to follow the dust swirls on the horizon. Talk of women and courting made his muscles tense. He'd done his fair share of mingling with society while attending medical college at Harvard, but no female had stirred anything in him that he cared to pursue further.

He'd often wondered what sort of woman would finally hold his interest. He'd watched his fellow classmates attend socials and court the ladies, while he'd spent most of his time, when he wasn't in school, away from the hustle and bustle of the city.

What was he even looking for in a woman, not that he'd ever taken a serious look? The ladies in Boston were nothing like the women of the Tukudeka band of Shoshone Indians with whom he'd grown up. There simply wasn't a comparison between a native woman and those who'd been raised in white society. One wasn't better than the other, but they were worlds different. Finding a native woman to hitch up with had been out of the question when he'd decided to pursue a medical certificate in the east rather than carve out a living trapping in the remote mountains his parents called home.

Any woman who'd catch his eye would definitely have to be someone who could hold her own and not wilt or faint at the slightest provocation. She'd have to know her way around civilized society as well as feel confident in the wilderness. Someone like his mother. No woman could hold a candle to Aimee Osborne.

Matthew shrugged. He'd had no time to think about women and courting. His focus was on building a medical practice, now that he held his doctor's certificate. He could have practiced medicine without one, but, aside from his mother, he hadn't apprenticed with any another physician. Sadly, she wasn't recognized as a doctor by eastern standards.

"I suppose sitting in the lecture halls in medical college gave you no time to think about the softer gender," Zach continued.

Matthew smirked. "The only thing I learned during those lectures was how to hone my skills at patience and letting my mind wander while pretending interest. Mama taught me more about medicine and healing than I've ever learned from any of my professors. Any arguments I've raised against their so-called theories and methods were cast aside and rebuffed. I don't know how it is with law, but raising questions of the established medical practices isn't tolerated."

Zach laughed. "Maybe we should tell Mama to come back east with us and teach them how it's done."

"Mama wouldn't dream of leaving the Yellowstone." Matthew smiled. The thought of his mother ever leaving his father or coming east, away from her beloved mountains, was incomprehensible.

"Well, once you have your own practice, you can show everyone how to properly heal people, and perhaps even save a few lives in the process."

"That's what I'm hoping."

Matthew's attention drew back to the dust swirls on the horizon. He nudged with his chin, but before he could speak, Zach said, "I've been noticing that, too. What do you suppose it is? It's not a dust storm."

"Guess we'd better find out." Matthew kneed his horse into a lope, and Zach followed.

Their horses covered several miles fairly quickly, and Matthew squinted into the distance. "Looks like wagons." He reined his horse to a walk. "Seven, and several riders."

"Trappers heading back into the mountains with supplies?" Zach shot him an inquisitive look.

Matthew frowned. "Why would they take wagons rather than pack animals?"

"Well, whoever they are, they're heading the same direction we are. Maybe we should join them for a while."

"Boston's made you soft." Matthew grinned at his brother. "I remember a time when nothing worried you and Sam on our trips to Fort Raymond or St. Louis."

Zach shrugged, and returned his grin. "Who says it's my safety I'm worried about? Maybe I'm trying to look out for those folks up ahead."

Matthew's brows raised in a mocking challenge. Zach waved him off, and nudged his horse forward. In no time, they'd reached the caravan of covered wagons, each one pulled by a team of six mules. It certainly didn't look like a supply train for one of the fur companies, even if several of the riders wore buckskins and were outfitted for a season of trapping in the mountains.

A few of the men who rode horses looked like they'd come fresh from the city. Matthew shook his head. What were a bunch of greenhorns doing out in the middle of nowhere, in hostile Indian territory? The Lakota and Cheyenne were friendly enough, but the Pawnee and Arikara had always made sport of trappers passing through the plains and heading into the mountains. A wagon train like this was easy pickings for those warriors. His frown deepened when a dark skirt fluttered from one of the wagon seats.

"What the hell?" he mumbled under his breath. Zach looked his way, just as surprised.

"I heard someone say at Fort Williams that there was a group of missionaries in the area, heading over the Rockies," Zach said.

"Missionaries?" Matthew couldn't keep the condescension from his question.

"Heading for the Washington Territory."

"Someone ought to have told them to turn around. They're going to get killed before they even get to the mountains." He shifted in the saddle, and glanced toward the wagon where he'd seen a woman's skirt flapping in the breeze. "And they're bringing women, too?"

Two riders broke away from the group, and headed their way. One was dressed in furs and skins, while the other wore black trousers, a black jacket over a white shirt, and a black hat he held onto while guiding his horse toward them.

"Might be wise to stick with them for a while, like I said," Zach mumbled as they waited for the two to approach. "Make sure they don't lose their scalps just yet."

"Well, I'll be," the one man dressed in buckskins shouted, and raised his hand. "If it ain't the Osborne twins. Still can't tell the two of you apart."

He brought his horse to a stop in a swirl of dust, and leaned forward in the saddle. His smile exposed several missing teeth. He adjusted his fur cap on his head, then extended his hand.

"Fitzpatrick," Matthew greeted, leaning over his own horse to reach for the man's hand.

"We ain't got nothin' to worry us over from these two," the trapper Matthew recognized as Thomas Fitzpatrick said to the well-dressed man who'd pulled his horse up alongside. "Would sure like to have you join us if you're heading west." He shot eager eyes at Matthew, then at Zach.

"Those don't look like supply wagons," Matthew said, gesturing with his chin toward the caravan.

The woodsman rubbed at his grizzled chin. "Them's not supply wagons. A few of us is taking Mr. Witmer here, his family, and a few others as far as rendezvous. They's missionaries, heading across the mountains."

Matthew assessed the man Fitzpatrick had called Witmer. His clothes were too clean for the wilderness, his salt and pepper beard neatly trimmed. His gloved hands held the reins of his horse as if he'd just learned how to ride a short time ago. How had this man, and the rest of these folks, managed to get this far without getting killed already? They belonged in the wilderness about as much as his father belonged in a fancy Boston parlor.

"Isaac Witmer." The man raised his chin, and extended

his hand to Zach, who shook it. "You are welcome to join us."

Matthew caught the quick glance his brother shot him. "You're a very trusting man, Mr. Witmer."

The older man smiled. "I like to believe that all men are good," he said.

Matthew coughed to hide the smirk he couldn't suppress. His initial assessment had been correct. This man wasn't going to last long in the wilderness. And he'd brought his family?

"Where's rendezvous this year?" Matthew directed his question at Thomas Fitzpatrick. At least these people had chosen wisely when they picked him as their guide. Not all trappers and woodsmen were as trustworthy. If Fitzpatrick led this missionary group, it wouldn't be a long stretch to assume that William Sublette and Jim Bridger were also among the men who accompanied them. They were all experienced mountain men, and Matthew would trust them with his life.

"Rendezvous along the Bighorn, in the Wind River Basin. Figure we're a couple weeks out from there."

"We'll join you," Zach said, before Matthew could say they'd go along at least that far. Obviously, his brother was of the same mind as he that these people needed all the help they could get.

Fitzpatrick nodded in satisfied approval. "Straight shot up to the Yellerstone from there," he said. "Assuming you're headed home to your folks' place."

"We are," Matthew confirmed, and reined his horse in the direction of the caravan. He glanced up at the late-afternoon sky as he led the way toward the group of wagons that had stopped. It was nearly time to make camp for the night. The lack of trees in the area would make it difficult for such a large group to find any cover.

"What do you plan to accomplish in the wilderness, Mr. Witmer?" Zach asked. Matthew turned his head slightly to listen.

"We're going to build a mission in the Washington Territory, and bring some civilization to the Indians." The man's voice was filled with enthusiasm.

Matthew's hands tightened around his reins. He'd seen and heard enough of men in Boston who were eager to reform the people who made this vast wilderness their home. No doubt as more men tried to sway the Indians to the European culture, it might only stir up trouble. The trappers had enough problems with hostile tribes.

"Where did you say you make your home, Mr. Osborne?"

"A remote area in the mountains along the Yellowstone," Zach answered evasively. Matthew breathed in relief. No doubt his brother was thinking the same thing as he. He didn't want these people coming to their valley. "Much further north than the direction you're heading," Zach added.

They reached the seven wagons just as one of the trappers shouted, "Time to bed down for the night. This is as good a place as any."

Matthew's lips twitched, when the tall man who had called out the order jumped from his horse. Jim Bridger. A good mountain man to camp with, but a teller of tall tales that would make anyone's head spin. Bridger glanced at him at that moment, and a wide smile spread across the trapper's clean-shaven face.

"Well, I'll be," he called. He yanked his hat from his

head, and slapped it against his buckskins. "The Osbornes. Ain't no use worrying about Pawnee from hereon." He rushed up to Matthew, and reached his arm up. Matthew leaned over his saddle, and shook his hand.

"Bridger." He nodded.

"Yes, sirree." Jim Bridger hopped from one foot to the other. He turned to face the rest of the group, and continued in a loud voice that matched his stature. "These two men here growed up in a place few men will ever see. Where the water runs so fast, the rivers boil, and fish can swim both sides of the Divide. Why, I once took a shot at an elk while I was there, but the critter didn't fall over dead. I shot it again, and again, but he just kept right on grazin'."

Jim Bridger glanced around, to see if he had a captive audience. He held up his hands, mimicking shooting a rifle, and crouched as if he were stalking prey. Matthew rolled his eyes. He'd heard this story many times.

"Well, now, as I got closer to the elk, I ran headlong into a mountain of glass. It was so clear, I could see right through it, and the elk on the other side."

"Obsidian may be smooth like glass, but you can't see through it." Zach leaned toward Matthew, and murmured. He'd dismounted his horse, and, thankfully, slapped Bridger on the back to divert his attention away from his tale.

Matthew glanced at the wagons. Men climbed down from the seats, and started to unhitch their teams. Mr. Witmer rode to one of the rigs, and helped a woman from the seat. Matthew caught a glimpse of auburn hair from underneath the white cap that covered her head. The plain, charcoal dress she wore didn't distract from her loveliness. She reached into the wagon, and helped another girl down from the tailgate. The two smiled at each other, then the first one's head turned. Matthew's breath caught in his throat.

A strong nudge to his arm diverted his attention from staring at her.

"She'd give Miss Halsey quite the competition." Zach leaned toward him and whispered in his ear. He looked toward the young woman, and nodded. "Her dress may be a bit plain, but she's definitely more attractive than Miss Halsey. Yup, might be an interesting journey to the Wind River."

Laughing, Zach led his horse to where the group of trappers set up their camp, leaving Matthew standing and swearing under his breath.

CHAPTER THREE

"Can you get a fire started, Mary? Father will want his supper shortly."

Della Witmer forced a smile to appear cheerful in front of her little sister. The strain of this journey was taking its toll on Mary. She looked tired most of the time. Della was tired, too. Tired of her tense relationship with their father. She tried her best not to let it show in front of Mary, who didn't need to be subject to that, even if she was aware of it.

"Of course, Della." Mary nodded, and scurried off to look for buffalo chips.

A twinge of guilt nagged at Della for sending her sister to take care of this unpleasant task. Since there were few trees in the area, the trappers who were their guides had shown them how to build fires out of dried-out bison dung. Apparently, it's what the Indians who lived in this desolate land utilized.

"Adelle."

Della whipped her head around. She'd just reached into the back of the wagon to retrieve supplies for making biscuits, when her father's sharp voice cut into her thoughts. She gritted her teeth, and inhaled a slow, calming breath. She pushed some wayward strands of hair under her day cap.

"Yes, Father?" She faced the stout man.

"I want you and your sister to remain close to the wagon from hereon." The piercing stare her father shot at her might make men in his congregation go weak in the knees, but Della raised her chin.

"We've always stayed close to the wagon," she said. "It's what you've commanded us to do since we started this journey. There are times, however, when we need to collect fire material, or have need for some privacy."

Isaac Witmer took a step toward her, his face turning red. "Don't get insolent with me. I can still raise the switch to you."

"Yes, Father." Della dropped eye contact, not because he'd intimidated her, but because she didn't want to cause another scene like what had happened a few weeks ago when they'd left the trapper outpost of Fort Williams. None of the mountain men had dared come close to her or her sister after her father's rant when she'd offered the men coffee.

If he was so concerned for their virtue, why hadn't he simply left her and Mary behind with their deceased mother's family in New York? The mountain men had been nothing but polite and respectful. She'd strained her ears to listen to their tales of adventure and danger each night, and would give anything to sit at their fire to hear more of their stories. Jim Bridger's accounts had been most entertaining, even if she didn't believe any of them.

Della's father stepped up next to her, and wrapped his hand around her upper arm, forcing her to look at him.

"Two more men have joined our caravan, and, although I trust that they are honorable, it won't do to have you or your sister carousing with the likes of them."

Della gritted her teeth. Her father trusted strangers more than he did his own daughters. Neither she nor Mary had ever given him cause to mistrust them in any way. She'd been a devoted daughter, but the urge to pull free of her father's tight hold on everything that she did had become stronger over the last few years.

Isaac Witmer had always demanded complete obedience from his wife and daughters, and while her mother may have bowed to his every wish without question, Della'd had enough. She was of age to make her own way in life, yet with her mother's passing, she'd stayed to take care of her sister, who was more like their mother – demure and obedient.

She laughed silently. Not that she'd had the means to leave. Over the years, her father had scared away any potential suitor who might have shown an interest, even respected members of his church congregation.

Her father released her arm. "Make sure you stay by the wagon, and your sister, too." He turned to walk away, then paused. "And keep your hair under your cap. We've come here to civilize the indigenous people, not turn into them."

Della expelled the breath she'd been holding after her father walked away. "Yes, Father," she mumbled, and continued to rummage through her food supplies.

Mary returned with buffalo chips and lit a pile on fire several yards from the wagon. Solomon Allen had unhitched her father's team of mules, and nodded curtly before leading the animals away from camp to find a grazing spot for the night. Della mixed together flour and lard with some water, and shaped the dough into biscuits that she placed into a dutch oven and set near the flames.

Boisterous laughter came from one end of camp, where the trappers had set out their bedrolls. The five men whom her father had enlisted as guides sat around their fire, along with the two newcomers. Della had only caught a glimpse of them when they rode into camp.

Dressed similarly to the trappers, the two men didn't look quite as rough around the edges as Mr. Thomas Fitzpatrick, or Mr. Jim Bridger and the others. Their clothes, while consisting of leather britches and hunting jackets over homespun cotton shirts, weren't as worn. Some of the mountain men's shirts looked as if they had been sewn together and repeatedly patched, and she'd go so far as to say that none of the material of the original shirt remained.

Della cast discreet glances toward the trappers while she prepared the evening meal for her father and sister. If only their wagon was closer, so she could hear their stories. No doubt new tales were being spun, now that their number had increased.

"They are handsome, aren't they?"

Della nearly dropped her wooden spoon at her sister's words. She straightened from leaning over the fire and stirring the beans in the pot.

"Whatever makes you say that?" she whispered. "If

Father heard you talk like that, he'd take the switch to your backside."

Della glanced at her sister, and her lips twitched. Mary dropped her gaze, and even in the dimming evening light, her cheeks visibly turned rosy. That her little sister had even noticed a man's looks had come as a complete surprise.

"I'm nearly sixteen, Della. Don't tell me you haven't taken notice of them yourself. And there are two of them."

Della couldn't suppress her smile any longer. "You're too young for wandering eyes," she chided in a whisper. She cast a hasty glance over her shoulder toward the men. "But yes, you're right. They are rather handsome."

Curious was the fact that these two men resembled each other almost as if they were mirror images. Their sandy-colored hair, while falling to their shoulders, didn't appear to be as tangled and unkempt as the others. They'd obviously spent some time in civilized society.

One of them sat cross-legged in the dirt by the fire. He bit off a chunk of something in his hand, and grinned broadly at whatever Mr. Bridger had said. As usual, he spoke in an animated fashion, holding everyone's attention. The man's companion, undoubtedly his twin brother, lay a little further away from the fire. His legs were stretched out in front of him, and he propped his torso on his upper arm. He wore a much more serious look than the other one.

Della sucked in a hasty breath of air and quickly turned her attention on her spoon when the man's eyes drifted her way. The split-second eye contact jolted her as if she'd burned her hand on a hot kettle. Her heart slammed against her ribs. She stuck the spoon back in the pot, and stirred its contents with exaggerated force, spilling some of the beans over the side. She willed her eyes to remain on the fire rather than look over her shoulder again to see if he was still looking her way.

"Go and tell Father that supper is ready," she said, and swiped a hand along her forehead. "And no more talk of handsome men," she added as an afterthought.

When her sister did as she'd asked, Della straightened, and turned her head again. Even with her back turned, the sensation that she was being watched overpowered her, sending tingles down her spine. It was as if the man's stare beckoned her to look his way again. Sure enough, he still had his eye on her. She swallowed past the lump in her throat, and straightened fully. Raising her chin, she held his stare. The man's lips widened slightly in a challenging smile, then he turned his attention to his companions.

Della smirked. He'd tried to intimidate her. Hopefully she'd sent a clear message that she wasn't so easily frightened. After wiping her hands on her apron, she spooned food onto a plate and handed it to her father when he walked up. He nodded curtly, and left again to sit with the men he'd brought along to help him build his mission. Thank the Lord he hadn't told her that she had to cook for them. While none of the men had brought families, they were responsible for their own meals.

She offered a plate to her sister, and joined her in a silent meal on the tailgate of their wagon. Della strained her ears to listen to what the mountain men were saying. A few of the missionaries had joined the trappers around their fire. Jim Bridger was boisterous as usual, and his voice carried through the camp, even drowning out the chirping of the crickets in the evening air.

"You just ask Zach and Matthew here if I'm tellin' the truth. They've lived up along the Yellerstone all their life, and they can tell ya all firsthand that I ain't lyin'. Ain't that right?" He nudged the man sitting next to him. The one lying away from the fire shook his head slightly.

"Why, ya only need to cast your fishing line in the lake, and by the time ya pull the trout out, it'll be cooked and ready to eat," he croaked. The men around him shook their heads and laughed.

"It's the gospel truth, I tell ya," Bridger roared. He glanced at the newcomer sitting next to him. "Tell 'em, Zach."

The man he'd addressed straightened, and rubbed his hand along his chin. Della set her plate on the tailgate and cocked her head to the side to hear, but the man didn't speak as loudly as Mr. Bridger, and his response was lost to her. Disappointed, she finished her meal, and scraped her plate clean.

Darkness came quickly, and the camp fell quiet. The trappers had warned them since they'd left Fort Williams to keep the fires low, and to speak softly once night set in. Everyone had been warned of the Pawnee, that an encounter with them might be dangerous. Even Mr. Bridger had to curb his habit of talking in a loud tone. The mountain men took turns standing guard throughout the night, and in the time since leaving the trading post, they hadn't encountered any Indians.

After packing away the food, Della glanced to where her father still sat with his men. She needed some time away from camp, the darkness and solitude away from the wagons beckoning to her. If she snuck away for just a few minutes, she'd be back before her father even noticed.

"I'll be right back, Mary. I need a little privacy."

Mary shot her a quick look, then glanced to where their father sat. She nodded, and Della smiled in thanks. Her little sister knew that she snuck off to be by herself for a few minutes each evening, and had kept her secret from their father.

Beyond the shadows of the campfires, Della stopped. She inhaled deeply. She hugged her arms around her waist, and stared up at the clear night sky, marveling at all the stars. Crickets chirped, and a desert wolf howled somewhere in the distance. A twig from one of the low-growing prairie bushes snapped nearby, and Della froze.

"Not wise to leave camp after dark," a low voice said from behind her.

Della spun around. The faint outline of a man with broad shoulders and a tall stance materialized out of the darkness. She strained her eyes. Although only his silhouette was visible, he was definitely one of the newcomers.

"Are you following me?" she asked, lifting her chin.

He chuckled softly. "Nope. I was already here. First turn at night watch."

Della swallowed her growing apprehension. Was this the same man who'd dared her with his challenging stare earlier, or was it the other one, who'd laughed with Mr. Bridger? Something told her he was the former. She glanced quickly toward camp, then back to the woodsman. If her father found out that she was alone in the company of a man, there was no telling what he might do.

"Is it true what Mr. Bridger said?"

Another quick chuckle rumbled in the darkness. "Which part?"

"I heard him say that you and – I assume – your

brother, live in the area he likes to tell stories about. Are they true?"

The sounds of the crickets seemed to grow louder while the man remained silent. Della was about to open her mouth to ask if he'd understood her question, when he spoke.

"Bridger likes to exaggerate and embellish his tales," he said. The rich timbre of his voice held her mesmerized. "He likes to mix the truth with his own versions."

"So which parts are the truth?" she pressed, eager to hear him speak some more. "Are there really rivers that boil and water that can shoot high into the air?"

There was another long pause before he answered. "I only know of one spot where there's a stretch of river hot enough that it could be considered boiling, but the water shooting into the sky is true. My folks call those things geysers."

"It sounds like a wonderful place." The images of such a phenomenon were lost to her.

"I don't think you'll be heading that way, Miss Witmer, and rightfully so. It's a harsh land, not for the faint of heart."

Della's eyes widened. First, because he knew her name, and second, had he just called her a weakling?

"I hardly think you're in the position to make that sort of judgment about my character, Mr. –"

"Matthew Osborne," he said in a low tone.

"Well, Mr. Osborne, as I was saying. I –"

"Adelle."

The sound of her father's booming voice sent a jolt of trepidation through her. She crossed herself mentally for the swear word that came to mind, one of the many she'd heard the trappers say out loud on several occasions.

"Thank you, for the warning about staying in camp, Mr. Osborne," she mumbled, and rushed off toward her wagon, bracing for her father's anger.

CHAPTER FOUR

Matthew reined his horse to a stop atop a shallow rise. The dark silhouettes of the *Paha Sapa,* the Black Hills, rose high into the cloudless sky in the distance. By tomorrow, they'd be out of Pawnee territory, and heading into the mountains that were sacred to the much friendlier Lakota.

For the last week, since joining the missionary caravan, he'd gotten little sleep. Always on alert from a possible Pawnee raid, he'd tossed in his bedroll unless it was his turn at night watch. Had it been just Zach and himself, or with the other trappers, his worries would have lessened. Seven wagons that stood out like a grizzly among a group of squirrels, however, were much more difficult to keep out of sight and harm's way.

Adding to his sense of unease were Isaac Witmer's daughters. Fending off a possible Indian raid would be easier if he didn't have to worry about the safety of a couple of females. Matthew focused his gaze into the distance. Once they reached the Wind River Basin, and the site of this year's trapper rendezvous, he and Zach would be parting ways with the wagons and heading north toward the Yellowstone. Then he could focus on other things again, and not think about further chance interactions with Miss Adelle Witmer.

Addy

Her sister called her Della, but when he'd first learned her name from Will Sublette, one of the trappers, he'd immediately thought of her as Addy. Not that he'd ever have the chance to call her by that name. Sublette had warned him that her father kept a watchful eye on both of his daughters, and none of the men were allowed to speak to them.

All week, Matthew had watched her from afar. She'd acted like a demure and quiet mouse in front of her father and around the other missionaries, keeping her head down and avoiding all eye contact. Yet when she thought no one was looking, she'd listen in on Bridger's wild tales, her eyes sparkling with keen interest.

A slow grin formed on his face. She hadn't backed down when he'd stared at her that first night, or when he'd told her the Yellowstone wasn't for the weak. He'd nearly intervened after she'd scurried off when her father called her back from wandering away from camp. Although he had a point, the man's angry outburst that she's been disobedient had boomed loudly through the night. Tom Fitzpatrick and Will Sublette had to give stern warning to stay quiet before Isaac Witmer calmed down.

Since then, Addy hadn't been alone for even a second. Her younger sister was constantly at her side. The faraway looks Matthew caught on her pretty face hadn't escaped his notice. He mentally shook his head. She was the most unlikely of women to catch his eye. He had no business talking to her.

Something about her demeanor, the way she'd stood up to him without flinching, and hadn't been intimidated by his outright stare, held his interest. If Witmer continued to keep her caged, he'd soon have a flighty deer on his hands that would escape at the first opportunity, rather than a devoted daughter.

Not that it's any of your concern, Osborne. She's heading west, and you're heading back east again after a winter with the folks.

Once they reached the Wind River, he'd never see her again.

"Another day, and I won't feel like a moving target anymore for a while, at least not until we reach Blackfoot Territory."

Matthew turned at Zach's words. His brother had pulled his horse up alongside, and stared off at the *Paha Sapa* as well. Crossing the endless flat prairie after leaving the Missouri River had always been the risky part of this journey. They'd made the trip with their parents since they were young boys, when his father traded furs in St. Louis.

Since the fur companies had come to the mountains and started holding annual rendezvous, the long trek was no longer necessary. Matthew, Zach, and their brother, Sam had continued to go as far as the Missouri nearly every summer to trade and bring back supplies to outfit the small trading post their parents had set up at their cabin. It was a familiar route for him, and they'd been in their share of skirmishes with the Pawnee, but this time, Matthew was on edge because of the caravan.

Because of the women . . . Because of one woman in particular.

"I'll be glad when we're in the mountains again," Matthew said.

He reined his horse around to head back to camp. Sublette had asked for volunteers this morning to go hunting for some fresh meat, and Matthew had happily offered. It had been a good excuse to get away from camp for a while and to clear his head. Zach, no doubt, had felt the same way, since he'd been more than eager to accompany him. Zach had shot a pronghorn, which now lay across his lap. It would be enough to feed everyone tonight and for several days.

"Another week or so, and we'll be parting ways with these good folks."

Matthew raised a questioning eyebrow at Zach's wide grin when he spoke.

"The quicker, the better," he grumbled. "I don't plan to stay at rendezvous. I doubt Mama and Papa will be there this year. They're expecting us along the Madison. We're already a week or more behind schedule. We would have made better time on our own."

Zach nodded. "But then you wouldn't have had the good fortune to meet Miss Witmer."

Matthew scoffed. His hand tightened on the reins. "What's that supposed to mean?" His brother's matchmaking efforts were getting downright infuriating. First it had been Miss Halsey, and now Isaac Witmer's daughter.

"I've seen the way you keep following her around camp." Zach sniggered.

Matthew straightened in the saddle. "I haven't been near the woman, nor do I plan on it anytime soon."

He hadn't gone near her, except for the one time that first night, but she'd been the one who had nearly walked into him in the dark. He hadn't been following her. He shifted his shoulder to ease the sudden tension in his neck. Talking to her had been a rather enlightening experience. She wasn't some mousy woman who'd faint at the first opportunity to draw attention to herself.

"Maybe you haven't been shadowing her physically, but your eyes have been following every move she makes. It's the first time I've ever seen you take such close notice of a woman."

Matthew glared at his brother. His scowl wouldn't intimidate Zach, but it gave him a small measure of satisfaction. "She's a missionary. Hardly a woman who would hold my interest."

"Her father's a missionary," Zach shot back calmly, holding his stare.

Matthew shook his head. Why was he even letting his brother goad him? "Seems to me that you're the one who's taken an unlikely interest in Miss Witmer."

Zach laughed. "No, just observing you. It's been rather entertaining, I must say, watching you look like some love struck moose these past days."

Matthew kneed his horse into a lope. This discussion only increased his tension. No one other than his brother knew him well enough to be this observant. He certainly hadn't let his fascination with Miss Witmer come to the surface for anyone else to see.

He followed the course of the shallow creek back toward where they'd left the caravan early this morning. With any luck, the wagons would have made at least a few miles' forward progress. The uneven terrain had slowed them down considerably. The landscape had gradually changed from flat prairie to greener meadows and a few hills over the last few days. Cottonwood, oak, and elm trees lined the creek bank they'd been following.

When Zach caught up to him, Matthew slowed his horse. No sense tiring out his animal to get away from his brother. All he had to do was ignore the teasing. His scowl remained, even if what Zach had said held some measure of truth.

Matthew groaned silently when Addy's words - her voice filled with awe and wonder when he'd spoken of the Yellowstone - came back to him. *"It sounds like a wonderful place."* How would she react if she could see and experience the wonders of the land where he'd grown up?

Zach abruptly pulled his horse to a stop, bringing a jolting halt to Matthew's wandering mind. He raised his hand in a warning gesture, and eased his mount behind a grove of cottonwoods. Dismounting, he checked his flintlock. Matthew followed without question. Zach wouldn't reach for his weapon without good reason.

Zach nudged with his chin in the direction they were heading. A dust cloud stirred in the distance. Matthew cocked his head to the side to listen. If he hadn't been daydreaming a moment ago, he would have heard the sound of a large group of horses' hooves nearby. Fast-moving horses, not the lumbering pace set by the mules pulling the wagons. Leaving their mounts behind, he and Zach made their way along the creek, using the trees and shrubs for cover. If shots had been fired, they would have heard them by now.

Apprehension and unease crept through Matthew the further they followed the creek upstream. The horses he'd heard were no longer on the move, but there was no doubt that they'd been in the general vicinity of the caravan, and their comrades. Not more than half a mile further along the stream, the wagons came into view. Zach hissed a curse close behind him.

A group of twenty-five Pawnee warriors surrounded the camp. Sublette and Bridger lowered their flintlocks, and appeared to be conversing with the leader. The missionaries stood by their wagons. Fitzparick and the other trappers remained with them.

Matthew's eyes instantly locked onto the Witmer wagon. A jolt of dread rushed through him. Addy stood by the wagon, while her sister sat in the driver's box. He motioned with his hand that he was going to move in closer.

Slowly, he made his way toward the camp. By all appearances, the wagons had stopped near the creek to rest. The Pawnee had obviously surprised them. Most likely, they'd been following the caravan for a while, and saw their opportunity.

Why hadn't they attacked? Matthew's fingers tightened around his flintlock. The Pawnee looked well-armed with rifles of their own, as well as bows and arrows. What he wouldn't give for his hornbow at the moment, but it was a weapon he only carried when he was home in the mountains.

When he crept close enough to hear, he crouched behind a dense willow shrub, and trained his rifle on the closest Pawnee. Zach silently followed. No words were needed between them. They'd wait and see what the Indians would do. It was a good sign that neither the Indians nor the trappers had fired a weapon. Sublette and his men were experienced with Indian encounters. If there was a chance to negotiate out of this predicament, they'd do it.

Witmer walked up to stand beside Bridger at that moment, while Bridger spoke in Pawnee. Addressing the man who appeared to be the leader, the trapper told him with quiet words and hand gestures that they were passing through in peace, and would be out of Pawnee hunting grounds in less than a day.

The Pawnee leader sat his horse proudly, his rifle across his lap, and he scanned the camp. Matthew tensed when the man's eyes lingered on the Witmer wagon. Zach must have felt the shift in him. He turned his head slightly, and shot him a warning glare. Matthew focused his attention on the camp, his fingers tingling near the trigger of his flintlock.

"We come in peace, and mean you no harm," Witmer spoke in a loud voice, stepping forward.

Bridger's arm reached out and held him back. One of the Pawnee who sat his horse next to the leader leaned toward him, and spoke quietly. Obviously, this warrior knew English, and was translating what Witmer had said. The Pawnee leader glared at Witmer with piercing eyes, and spoke in his native language.

"Show that you come in peace," Bridger translated. "They'll want you to offer gifts," he added.

Witmer smiled, then looked back at the leader. "We've brought seeds to grow crops, and tools to work the land as gifts, as well as the Good Book. While we wish to distribute them to the people further west where we intend to settle, we'd be happy to gift some to you as a token of our friendship."

Matthew suppressed a smirk. Zach shot him another warning sideways glance.

The other Indian tried to translate, but the word *book*, or what it meant, seemed to be lost to him.

"Offer them something they can use, like readily available food or clothing," Bridger said. "These Injun's are hunters. They don't grow crops."

Witmer's head snapped to the trapper. "We can't give up our food. We will provide them with means to grow their own."

He reached into his coat pocket. Several Indians raised their weapons at his gesture.

"Easy, Witmer. Your scalp might be worth a little more than a sack of flour," Sublette said.

"I was reaching for my Bible," the man retorted.

He stepped up to the Indian, and held out a black book. The Pawnee stared at it, but didn't take it. He shook his head. Witmer turned to look at Sublette and Bridger. Even from a distance, the anger and indignation rising to the man's surface was easy to see.

"What should I offer?" he called loudly. "We need our provisions to get us over the mountains." He spun around, and pointed at his wagon. "We have nothing else we can part with." He paused, then added, "What do they want? Would offering up my first-born daughter be enough?" His voice rose even more.

Matthew cursed under his breath, and would have crashed through the thick canopy of bushes he and Zach hid behind, if not for his brother's quick and firm hands on his arms, holding him back.

Loud talking in camp followed Witmer's outburst. The Indian who'd acted as interpreter translated Witmer's words to his leader, to which the Pawnee nodded. Several people talked at once, Witmer being the loudest.

"Ain't no use takin' back what you said," Bridger warned him, grabbing his arm.

"You can't be serious," the missionary raged. "I wasn't offering him my daughter."

"It's what he took it to mean," Sublette said. "If you refuse him now, we're all dead. We might take a few of them with us, but we're outnumbered."

"I'll go with them, if that's what it takes to make them leave the rest of you alone," Addy said boldly. She stared at her father, her eyes filled with fear, but her chin was raised and she stood tall.

Matthew strained against Zach's hold when Addy stepped forward. Her sister cried her name in panic.

"We're all dead if you rush in there," Zach growled against his ear. "We'll get her back, but not right now."

Matthew cursed repeatedly, his pulse throbbing at his temples. His brother was right. He stared toward the camp. Despite everything, something radiated inside him, staring at the woman who was willing to sacrifice herself for everyone else.

The Pawnee leader nodded, and leaned over his horse, reaching out his arm. Addy glanced over her shoulder at her sister, whose frantic calls pierced the air, then held out her hand, and the Indian pulled her onto his horse behind him. He raised his hand in the air, and with a loud whoop, kicked his horse into a run. His warriors followed, and the party rode off in a cloud of dust.

Matthew pulled his arm free from his brother's tight grip. He sprinted downstream to where he'd left his horse. Anger such as he'd rarely felt burned through his veins.

"We'll get her back," Zach repeated, matching Matthew's strides.

"If he hurts her in any way, that Pawnee is as good as dead."

Matthew swung up on his horse's back, and kicked it into a run, back toward camp. He'd get his anger under control first, and then he was going after the woman who'd just stolen his heart with her selfless act of bravery.

CHAPTER FIVE

Jim Bridger and the other trappers surrounded him and Zach when Matthew rode into camp.

"Pawnee came to call while you was gone. Took the Witmer girl. Was nothin' we coulda done. They was on us faster than flies on fresh bison dung," Bridger said excitedly.

Zach dropped the pronghorn he'd shot earlier to the ground, and dismounted. "We saw what happened," he said.

"And you did nothing?"

Matthew's head whipped around at Isaac Witmer's booming voice. The red-faced man shook visibly as he headed toward them from where he'd stood by his wagon. Several of his followers flanked him. His daughter, Mary, sobbed loudly from inside the rig.

Matthew threw his right leg over his horse's withers and landed lightly on his feet. The anger that had nearly made him act like an impulsive fool just minutes ago was gone, replaced with a calm determination. Witmer's accusation threatened to bring his rage back to the surface. He stared at the man as he strode toward him.

Matthew stopped just inches from the older man. He leaned forward, his eyes locked on Isaac Witmer. "What would you have suggested we do?" He sneered.

Witmer's mouth opened, then closed. His eyes widened. There was no anguish or pain displayed there, like a parent would show after having lost a daughter. He only looked enraged, no doubt because something had happened over which he'd had no control.

"If those Pawnee had known we were watching, they would have killed everyone in this camp. Even if we'd have been here, we were outnumbered." He lowered his voice slightly. "We're going to bring your daughter back."

Witmer stepped backward, nearly tripping. "Bring her back?" he stammered. "How can I ever look at her the same again? She won't be fit for civilized company after today."

Matthew's forehead scrunched. His jaw muscles tightened, and his entire body tensed. Forcing his arms to remain at his side, rather than grab hold of the man in front of him and shake some sense into him, he advanced on Witmer again.

"Not fit for civilized company?" he echoed. "She's your daughter. She sacrificed herself for everyone in this camp, including you, because of your stupidity."

Witmer's features hardened even more. He raised his chin. "Adelle has always had a rebellious streak in her. She's never wanted to conform. This will be her punishment for all her insolence over the years."

Matthew held back a curse at the unbelievable words coming from this man.

"The way you're trying to conform people to your beliefs and your ways may have worked where you're from, but it's not going to work out here. It's going to get you killed," he hissed. Matthew turned to walk away from Witmer. Another second, and his control would snap. "I'm going to bring her back."

Zach and the group of trappers hadn't moved, watching the exchange. Matthew headed toward them. Every inch of him screamed to get on his horse and follow that Pawnee raiding party, but experience told him to bide his time.

"If you succeed in bringing her back, she will not be welcome here. She will be your responsibility."

Matthew stopped in his tracks at Witmer's words behind him. His back stiffened, and he ground his teeth, then continued walking without glancing back.

"He's a hard one, ain't he?" Fitzpatrick said when Matthew joined the group of woodsmen. "Trying to preach to everyone, but might be better off following his own advice about trust and forgiveness." He looked from Matthew to Zach, and nodded. "What you two done, staying out of sight, was the right thing to do."

Bridger laughed. "They'da killed us all if you'd come ridin' in, and shootin' at 'em. At least this buys us some time before they come back. Sure was a brave thing that gal done."

Matthew's glance swept over his comrades, his gaze finally resting on Will Sublette.

"I'm going to go after Miss Witmer. I suggest you get these wagons moved as quickly as possible toward the mountains. Drive through the night if you have to, and find cover. Once I free her, the Pawnee will be back, and they'll be out for blood."

"I ain't convinced they won't be back, either way. They was merely taking our measure this time," Bridger said. "Pawnee don't just come for a social visit. Why, I remember one year, when me an' Hugh Glass --"

"Let's get these wagons moved," Sublette cut him off. "If Witmer doesn't want to comply and break camp, I ain't willing to stay here and be a sitting duck."

Matthew headed for his horse. His insides seethed with rage. Witmer was the kind of man who would get everyone killed. The man's last words haunted him. Matthew didn't doubt for a second that Addy's father meant what he'd said about not wanting her back.

She'll be your responsibility.

What was he going to do with Addy once he freed her?

"What's got you so determined about this woman?" Zach asked quietly, stepping up next to him. "I know I goaded you about her earlier, but I never thought you felt this strongly. You don't even know her."

Matthew held his brother's gaze. He inhaled a deep breath to calm the rage inside him over what had happened, and shook his head slightly. "Remember what Papa used to tell us about Mama? How they met?"

Zach nodded.

"How, from the moment he first saw her, he somehow knew that finding her was meant to be. That he felt an instant connection to her?" Matthew held his brother's stare before he elaborated. "I understand what he meant a lot better now. There's something about Addy that . . . I can't explain it. She caught my eye as soon as we rode into

Witmer's camp that evening." He smirked. "She's not someone I should even give a second's notice, but whatever's taken hold of me won't let go."

Zach's mouth widened in a slow smile. He nodded in understanding, even if the expression on his face conveyed that he didn't quite comprehend, but he would stand behind Matthew no matter what.

"Let's bring her back, then." Zach gave him a good-natured slap to the back.

Matthew's features hardened. He glanced over his shoulder. Bridger, Fitzpatrick, and the other trappers readied their horses, while Sublette had gone off to talk to Witmer.

"Isaac Witmer doesn't want her back. You heard him." He scowled.

"Who said anything about bringing her back to *him*?" Zach's brows rose. "I think the man's in shock at what happened. People talk in anger sometimes when, what's really going on, is that they're scared. But, if he truly doesn't want her, and if she's willing, we'll bring her with us up the Yellowstone."

Matthew's quick laugh earned him a few inquisitive stares from the men in camp. Hadn't he told the young lady that the likelihood of her seeing the Yellowstone region was slim to none? During the one time he'd spoken to her, she'd impressed him even then, with her challenging retort that he had no business judging her character. She'd proven already that she was far braver than she first appeared.

Matthew pulled his knife from its sheath, and checked its sharpness on a piece of rawhide. He did the same with his ax. His flintlock was loaded. He glanced at his brother.

"They won't hurt her," Zach said, a serious look on his face. "That was a hunting party. That's why they didn't attack. They might be days away from their village."

Zach's words were meant to reassure him. Matthew nodded. Once the Pawnee reached their main camp, Addy would find out her fate. She might get traded or sold to someone, or married off to one of the warriors. Until then, none of the men would touch her. His body tensed. He'd get her back before then.

"Bridger is right, though. They will be back, and not as a hunting party. I hope they can get these missionaries to safety before then."

"It all depends if those warriors feel brave enough to enter Lakota hunting grounds, or if they'll want to gather a stronger force. If the wagons move through the night, they'll have a good chance. Sublette and his men know what they're doing."

Matthew glanced toward camp when harnesses jingled, and wagon wheels creaked. He mounted his horse, and met the trappers who flanked the wagons.

"We'll catch up with you before you reach the Wind River," he said, holding out his hand to Will Sublette.

"You be careful. I don't want to have to head up to the Yellerstone to tell yer Pa that you lost yer scalp to a bunch of Pawnee."

Matthew grinned. He fell back, and waited for the Witmer wagon to roll past. Isaac Witmer shot him an icy stare. Matthew ignored it, and guided his horse up alongside to where Mary sat next to her father on the driver's seat. Her eyes were swollen and red.

He looked up at her. "I'll get your sister back."

She stared at him, and nodded, then cast a hasty glance

at her father. Mary lowered her head, her hands clasped tightly in her lap.

"One final word of advice, Mr. Witmer." Matthew glared at the man until he made eye contact. "Don't say something to an Indian, or in the presence of one, unless you absolutely mean it. I hold you accountable for what happened to your daughter, and you ought to be proud of her for what she did. She's a brave woman, and every man in this outfit should be thanking her for her selfless act."

Without waiting for a reply, he reined his horse away from the wagon, and fell back to where Zach waited for him by the creek. His gaze shifted into the distance, in the direction where the Pawnee had gone.

The shallow stream they followed soon flowed into a wider, fast-moving creek, and the terrain changed from flat to more mountainous. Deep gullies slowed them down considerably, and large stretches of cottonwoods and shrubs obstructed their view. The creek widened into a river, which had carved out a steep and narrow ravine, making it impossible to ride close to the water.

"It'll be too dark to follow their tracks soon," Zach observed.

"But also easier to spot their camp. They'll have stopped for the night somewhere."

Matthew glanced down the rocky embankment, the water rushing loudly below. He leaned over his horse, and studied the tracks in the soil. Something wasn't right.

The vegetation here was trampled. It appeared as if the warriors had stopped in this spot. No one had dismounted their horses, so perhaps they had held some kind of quick discussion amongst each other. Where there had been dozens of horse prints before, a few had veered away from the main group, while the rest continued in the same direction they had gone.

Matthew raised his head, and scanned the nearby trees. The hair at the nape of his neck rose. He cast a quick look at his brother, who had also fallen silent. Zach raised his rifle, just as a loud war cry pierced the air. Matthew fired his flintlock at the same time as his brother. Two Pawnee fell from their horses. With practiced speed, he reloaded his weapon, and took aim at another Indian. An arrow flew past him, grazing his arm.

Matthew gritted his teeth, and swore under his breath. His rifle was too slow and useless to fend off this many warriors. He leapt from his horse and crouched near a rock, yanking his pistol from his belt. Zach had already done the same. Three warriors, their clubs raised, advanced on his brother. Matthew aimed, and fired. One Indian fell from his horse. Zach swung at another one with his rifle, using it as a club, bringing down one of his attackers.

Matthew dropped his pistol, and ripped his knife from his belt, then charged. Loud thunder of hooves echoed behind him, and a sudden, sharp pain to his back halted him in his tracks. He fell forward, landing hard on the rocky terrain. A triumphant whoop rang in his ear. He braced his hands in the dirt to stand, when a moccasined foot kicked him in the gut. The air left his lungs, and Matthew rolled to the side from the impact.

Somewhere in the distance, Zach called his name. A thousand thoughts raced through Matthew's head as his body made impact with the ground. The arrow in his back sent searing pain through him.

When the Pawnee advanced again, Matthew kicked

out with his leg, sending the warrior to the ground. Groping for the knife he'd dropped, he clamped his hand around the handle, and threw it.

Breathing hard, Matthew raised himself up off the ground. Another warrior came at him, his war club raised. He ducked to avoid the blow, and staggered backward. The ground beneath him gave way. His head shot up. More warriors than he could possibly fend off surrounded Zach.

"Zach," Matthew called weakly, just as he lost his footing. He fell over the embankment, tumbling down the ravine. Sharp rocks battered and jarred him. His body hit the frigid water as loud war cries screeched from above.

Matthew gulped in a deep breath. The cold water quickly numbed the pain from the arrow in his back, and he clawed his way toward shore while the strong current swept him further downriver.

"Zach," he rasped. Dammit. What was happening with his brother? By now, the Pawnee would have killed him. He'd been lucky enough to fall down the ravine, but not Zach.

The Pawnee war cries stilled, until there was only the sound of the rushing water over rocks. Matthew groped his way up the rocky shore, beneath some branches that reached into the water, and pulled himself from the frigid river. Bracing his hands in the dirt, he pushed his upper body off the ground. Renewed pain shot through his back, and he sank down into the soil beneath the vegetation.

He had to pull that arrow out of his back, but his arms were too weak to cooperate. His last conscious thought was of his brother. A sinking feeling of sorrow engulfed him. He'd failed to help Zach.

What seemed like an eternity later – or was it happening now - a woman's voice echoed somewhere in the deep recesses of his mind. It was a voice he'd longed to hear. She called his name, beckoning him back from the darkness that threatened to consume him.

CHAPTER SIX

Della sat against a tree, her knees pulled tightly under her skirts. After a heart-stopping ride for several hours over rough terrain, she'd breathed a sigh of relief that she'd been allowed to get off the horse's back. Her legs had barely supported her when she'd stumbled to the tree.

While astride the horse, she'd clung to the Indian who'd agreed to take her in trade for leaving peacefully. Now, however, she couldn't get far enough away from him. After her father's impulsive outburst, she'd seen no other way out of the situation but to agree to go with the Pawnee.

Renewed fear gripped her for her sister, her father, and all the men in their company. The Indians had stopped shortly before arriving at this spot, and had talked excitedly. They'd come to some sort of a decision. The leader had handed her over to one of the men who were with her now, and all but these two warriors had ridden off in a different direction. What if they had gone back to kill everyone, after all? Her sacrifice would have been in vain, and she would much rather die at her sister's side.

The two Indians who'd been left behind ignored her completely. One gathered branches while the other tethered their horses. She glanced discreetly toward her two guards. If they thought she'd just sit there because she'd willingly come with them, they could think again.

The trappers had looked shocked at her father's words, even if everyone but the Indians seemed to know he hadn't been serious. Her father had a reputation for saying things in the heat of the moment that he took back as soon as he calmed down. Della had realized instantly that this had been one time when he couldn't take his words back. There was no doubt in her mind that the Pawnee would have killed them all had she not agreed to her father's off-handed remark.

Fully aware of what was going to happen to her when she'd agreed to go with the Indians, she hadn't given it a second thought. Her faith was strong, and it would get her through this. It had kept her calm all this time.

She laughed quietly. How often had she wished for someone to come along and free her from her father's controlling hand? Never had she imagined that this would be the manner in which she'd leave him. Just like she hadn't wanted her father to decide her future, her fate was not going to be decided by some Pawnee warrior, either. Somehow, she'd figure out what to do.

Several shots rang out in the distance. Her two guards looked up, and talked excitedly. They appeared as puzzled as she was at the sound, and looked toward her. One of them untethered his horse, and rode from their camp.

Della held the other man's stare. Was he thinking the same thing as she – that someone had come to try and rescue her? Her heart beat faster at the thought. She turned her head away from the man's glaring eyes, and glanced at the ground. Rocks large enough to cause injury to a man were scattered around in abundance.

Could she do it? She swallowed the lump in her throat.

She'd done a lot of things she never would have dreamed of since leaving the security of New York months ago. Wandering away from camp in the darkness to find a few moments to herself, for instance, was one of them. Not to mention talking to a complete stranger while alone in the dark. Or, her fascination with the stories the mountain men told. Her father had said that this journey would be safe, but she'd seen early on that the wilderness beyond the Missouri was not a place for weak individuals. Every day had been a trial in some way or another, but this was her most difficult test of courage yet.

Matthew Osborne's words, telling her that where he called home was no place for people like her, had remained with her since he'd said them. This was a true test to see if he'd been right. She hadn't ever considered herself a weakling, but hurting another person was more than she wanted to do to prove her bravery.

They will hurt, and most likely kill you, if you don't do it first.

She mentally shook her head. She couldn't kill anyone, but perhaps she could hit him enough to incapacitate him so that she could get away. Imagining the handsome woodsman's face, as he challenged her with his stare and his words, gave her the courage she needed. Determination raced through her. She would prove that Matthew Osborne was wrong about her. She wasn't weak, and she was cut out for life in this harsh land.

The warrior quickly lost interest in looking at her, and continued to build his fire. Keeping one eye on the Indian, she reached for several good-sized stones. Making an impulsive decision, Della stood, and walked toward him. She eyed the horse tethered a few paces to his right. If she could get to the animal, she could make her escape better than on foot.

The Indian glanced up from his task. Della swallowed, and sucked in a breath for courage. She tightened her grip around the rock she held in her hand. She'd never physically hurt another person in her life. Could she even go through with it?

The Indian straightened, and stared at her. She was close enough now that she couldn't miss. He would never see it coming. It was now or never. If David could fell a giant with a stone, perhaps she could, too. Della swung her arm, and threw the rock.

She held her breath when her missile connected with the Indian's head. Stunned, he stumbled backward, but to her horror, he didn't fall. Anger blazed in his eyes. He touched a hand to his head, then advanced on her with bared teeth. The meaning of his harsh words, although she didn't understand them, was perfectly clear. She'd had one chance, and she'd lost.

Della stumbled backward as he advanced on her. She fumbled for another rock from the pocket of her apron. The Indian ran at her, and grabbed her arm. She raised her hand that held the rock, and lunged forward. With a loud crack, she brought her weapon down against the back of his head.

The Indian's momentum brought her down to the ground with him when he fell. Della nearly screamed, but if she did, she might alert the other Pawnee. Pushing against the man's heavy body with all her strength, she pulled free of his weight, and scrambled to her feet. The smell of sweat mingled with the sweet scent of blood, and Della shuddered.

Her head shot up, looking to where this man's companion had gone, but all remained quiet. She ran toward the horse, then stopped, and turned. She rushed back to the Indian on the ground, her heart pounding so loud, she couldn't hear anything else around her. She muttered a quick prayer. Had she killed him?

She breathed as if she'd run for miles, her knees going weak with the thought. There was no time to dwell on it. He would have hurt her, or even killed her, had she not acted. She bent down, and pulled the knife from the man's belt at his waist. Her hand trembled when she stuck it in her pocket, careful not to cut herself. If the other warrior returned, she now had a weapon.

Her shaky legs carried her to the horse. Fumbling with the leather reins, she pulled it free from its tether, and led the animal to a nearby boulder large enough to step on to get onto the horse's back. Any moment now, the other Indian would return, and her efforts to escape would be for nothing.

Struggling with her skirts, she pulled herself onto the animal's back, and gripped with her knees. She held tight to the reins, and weaved her fingers in the horse's long mane. Giving it a kick, she urged her mount forward.

The horse obeyed, and galloped through the forest. Della leaned over its neck, and guided it as best she could in the direction from which they'd come earlier. The rushing sound of a creek nearby urged her on. If she could follow its course, it would lead her back to where the wagons had camped.

Della slowed the horse, keeping it close to the water's edge. She glanced in all directions. Any moment, the Pawnee would find her. The creek forked, and she paused. She hadn't paid much attention when they'd come through this area the first time. Which was the correct stream to follow? The Indians hadn't stayed this close to the water. They'd taken a route along the top of a deep gully. That's the way she needed to go, but nothing looked familiar.

Making a decision, she guided the horse into the water, and rode upstream a short distance. She crossed to the other side, and continued to head along the bank of the water. It soon became apparent that she'd chosen the wrong way. The landscape opened up to flat grassland if she continued heading in the direction she'd taken. Turning the horse, she rode through the water again, this time taking the other route at the fork in the creek.

Soon, the riverbank narrowed to where the horse had to splash through the water at times. Dense willows lined the edges of the river, and the sides of the ravine became too steep to move forward.

"Looks like we've made another mistake," she whispered to the horse, glancing upriver. Unless she wanted to swim, she needed to turn around. Was this why the Indians hadn't used the gully, but stayed at the top of the ravine?

Soon, it would be too dark to see anything. Night was quickly descending on her, and fear ripped through her. At least this was the correct way.

"Don't fall apart, Della," she said quietly to calm her growing apprehension. "Keep to the river, and you won't lose your way."

The horse snorted, as if in answer to her words. Its body tensed beneath her, and Della gripped him tighter by the reins. She'd heard the trappers talking that they trusted their horses more to alert them to danger than any of their comrades.

What was this horse so worried about? She leaned forward, and strained her eyes, looking at the dense bushes up ahead. Was that a man's foot sticking out from under one of the branches? Her heart raced. Was he dead? No one would lie like that and simply be asleep. He was too close to the water's edge. If it was a dead person, perhaps he had things that might be of some use to her.

You might have killed a man earlier, and now you're going to steal from another?

A shudder passed through her. She made the sign of a cross, then slid from her horse's back. Leading him forward, she moved toward the willow bushes. Fumbling in her pocket, she grabbed the knife tightly in her hand. A moccasin became more visible the closer she approached, but it hadn't moved. Her palms began to sweat.

"Hello?" she called, her voice faint and quivering.

A deep groan answered. She froze. This man was alive! When he didn't move, she inched forward. She dropped the horse's reins, and pushed some of the branches aside. Her heart dropped to her stomach.

A man - a white man - dressed in soaked buckskins,

lay face down in the dirt beneath the willow. An arrow stuck out of one side of his lower back. Something familiar struck her about this man. His damp, shoulder-length hair appeared darker than it would be once dry. Della rushed beneath the willow, and dropped to her knees.

"Mr. Osborne?" she said, touching the man's shoulder. He groaned again, and stirred. "Please, Mr. Osborne, tell me what to do to help you."

Tears filled her eyes, and panic flooded her. The red fabric of his homespun shirt shocked her a second time. Matthew Osborne! For a week she'd been more aware of him than she'd ever been of another man in her life. He'd kept his distance since their brief encounter that first night, but that hadn't prevented her from casting discreet glances in his direction whenever he'd been nearby in camp. The only way she'd been able to tell him apart from his brother was the red color of his shirt. Zach Osborne wore a tan shirt.

The man shifted, and groaned again. He raised his head slightly, and his eyes opened. A faint smile, or perhaps it was a grimace, formed on his lips.

"Addy," he rasped, his voice weak and barely audible.

Della leaned in closer to hear him better. Who was Addy? Was he delusional? Perhaps he had a wife by that name. She didn't dwell on why this thought disturbed her.

"What can I do, Mr. Osborne?" she asked again, close to his ear.

"Who else is with you?"

She shook her head. "No one. I'm alone."

He stared at her for, what seemed like an eternity. He groaned again before he spoke.

"Get that arrow out of my back." His words were stronger, but still forced, and laced with pain.

Della straightened. She swallowed. "How?" she squeaked.

Matthew Osborne opened his eyes wider, and stared up at her. "I was wrong about you," he said.

Her own eyes widened. Who was he talking about? He smiled again. It was definitely a smile this time. Della's heart melted, and her limbs weakened.

"I . . . I beg your pardon?" she stammered.

"You're not weak. You're a brave woman." He chuckled softly. "And I'm dying to know how it is that you're here, but first I need you to get that arrow out of my back."

"I've never--"

She tensed when his hand snaked up and grabbed her wrist. His smile had vanished, and his stare rooted her to the spot.

"Strip some bark off these willow trees, the driest you can find, and pound them into powder." He stopped to catch his breath. "Then find some soft dirt, and mix it together with the powder and some water to make a paste. Once you have that ready, pull the arrow out, and cover the hole with the paste. Be ready, because it's gonna bleed a lot."

Della gaped at him, then nodded. She had no time to think. She merely did what he asked, and returned to his side minutes later, a thick mass of dirt and willow bark powder in her hands. She knelt beside him. He remained motionless. Had he passed out, or died?

"Mr. Osborne, I'm back with the paste," she whispered, and tentatively touched his shoulder. The firm muscles beneath her fingers bunched, sending tingles up her arm.

"Good girl," he rasped. "It's getting dark. You'd better make it quick, and then we need to be gone from here."

Della nodded, swallowing her apprehension. If she could hit one man over the head with a rock, surely she could pull an arrow from another man's back to save his life. A chill raced down her spine at the thought of what she was about to do.

"Do it. I know you can," he said with firm conviction in his voice.

Della tightened her lips, and wrapped her hands around the wooden shaft of the arrow. She tugged, but it didn't budge.

"It won't come out," she squeaked.

"Pull quick, and pull hard," Matthew said, his voice laced with pain.

Della inhaled several deep breaths. She met his hard stare, then wrapped her hands around the shaft again. With a swift jerk upward, she pulled as hard as she could. Matthew tensed beneath her, then expelled a long breath, but he didn't make any other sound. Sweat covered his face, and he grimaced. He helped when she pulled his leather hunting jacket and shirt up his torso, and quickly pressed the paste she'd made over the bleeding wound.

"You need a bandage," she said, and stood on trembling legs. Lifting her skirt, she tore a large strip of material from her petticoat. "Can you sit up?"

Matthew raised himself to a sitting position. His breathing was labored, a telltale sign that he was in pain. Della marveled at this man's self-control. He held his clothing up while she wrapped the cotton material around his lower torso. When she leaned in to reach around his back, his warm breath against her cheek sent renewed ripples of awareness through her. She'd never been this intimately close to a man before.

"We need to get away from this area," he said quietly. "Before the Pawnee find us."

"I have a horse," she answered quickly. Matthew stared up at her. The fleeting look of wonder that passed through his eyes turned her legs to pudding.

When he stood, rather unsteady for a moment, she reached her hand out to help.

"Let's go," he said, leading the way out from under the willow bushes.

"How will you know where to go?" Della asked. "It'll be too dark to see anything in mere minutes."

"I need you to trust me." He reached for the Indian pony's reins, and locked his gaze on her.

Della stared up at him. His dark eyes appeared even darker in the dim light. Sudden clarity jerked her, like nothing ever had. She nodded. "I do trust you," she whispered.

CHAPTER SEVEN

Della sat behind Matthew on the horse. She wrapped her arms around him to keep her balance, just as she'd done with the Pawnee who'd taken her away from her family. This time, however, she wasn't afraid, nor did it bother her to be this close to a man. In fact, nothing had ever given her the kind of tingling sensations and heart flutters as she experienced now.

Matthew Osborne urged the horse through the river, the water deep enough in places to reach past the animal's belly. Della's shoes and skirts soaked up the water, and her toes turned numb from the cold. The woodsman didn't speak, and so she kept quiet, too. The night had enveloped them completely when he guided the horse to the opposite shore. The only light came from a partial moon casting silvery reflections on the rippling water.

The horse lurched forward to scramble up the embankment, and Della's grip around Matthew tightened. He stiffened slightly, and she eased her hold around him, and clamped her legs more firmly around the animal's belly instead.

"I'm sorry," she stammered. Had she aggravated his injury?

He didn't say anything, but kept the animal moving forward. Della's thigh muscles burned from the long hours of straddling a horse all day. She fought back tears for all that had happened, and exhaustion threatened to overtake her. When the horse rocked forward a second time, her body jerked in another direction. She lost her grip, and would have fallen, if Matthew Osborne's hand hadn't reached back to steady her.

"Just a bit further and we'll rest." His quiet, yet commanding voice sent a surge of hope and reassurance through her.

If he could ride through the night, injured as he was, then she had nothing to complain about. Della readjusted her position on the animal's back in an effort to minimize contact with him.

"Hold on to me."

"I don't want to hurt you," she stammered. Her fingers wrapped around the rawhide material of his hunting coat, careful not to touch him directly. She'd clung to him without any forethought about what she was doing earlier, other than trying to remain on the horse. Now that he was talking to her, her face heated from her actions.

Mr. Osborne still held her arm from where he'd steadied her a moment ago. He released it, and took hold of her hand instead, bringing her arm around his middle.

"Hold on to me, like before. We're heading uphill, and I

don't need you sliding off," he grumbled, his voice laced with pain.

Della's heart pounded faster, sure that he could feel it. He held firm to her hand, pressing it against his abdomen. Reluctantly, she brought her other arm around him, and interlocked her hands. She had no choice but to pull herself fully against his back.

Her grip tightened when the horse moved up a steep incline until it leveled out. She focused on the faint dark outlines of trees and more hills once they reached the top of the ravine, rather than on the solid feel of the man to whom she clung. He kept the horse at a steady pace, leading into the trees, and Della's eyes grew heavy from lack of sleep, and all that had happened today.

"Addy, wake up."

The deep voice close to her ear startled Della from dozing. She sat up straighter, and momentary fear rushed through her in the complete darkness. A shiver raced down her spine when something swooshed above her, and an owl hooted.

"We're stopping here, so you can rest," he added.

"Here?" she asked, groping for consciousness.

Mr. Osborne loosened her hands from around his middle, and dismounted the horse. She scrambled off the animal's back, keeping her hands on the horse to steady herself.

"There's good cover here among the trees."

He took hold of her hand, and led her through the darkness. Heat ran up her arm from his firm grip on her.

"I can't see anything," she whispered.

"Your eyes will adjust. I can't start a fire for you, but you can put this on, to keep warm."

He released her hand, and placed something around her shoulders. Her body instantly relaxed into the warmth that enveloped her. The smell of rawhide and wood smoke surrounded her - the scent of the man she'd come to know so intimately for the last few hours. How long had it been since they'd left the river?

"What about you? You're injured," she protested, looking toward where his face ought to be.

"I've had worse," he said, his tone strained.

"I can hear it in your voice that you're in pain, Mr. Osborne. A little cold won't bother me, but what if you get feverish?"

He let out a long breath. "Wait here under these trees, and get some rest. I'll be fine."

Della reached out her hand, which connected with a firm arm. "And what will you be doing?"

There was a lengthy pause. "Do you only argue with men after dark, or is that a daytime habit of yours, too?"

Della strained her eyes to see, but it was simply too dark to make out his features. Her lips tightened in a firm line. Why did all men have to be bossy and demanding? All her life, she'd had to put up with it from her father. Something was different about Matthew Osborne's demands, though. His tone didn't imply complete obedience, more like there was a sense of urgency to his demands.

"I'm not arguing. I'm simply stating a fact, and asking questions."

He removed her hand from his arm. "All right, then," he said. "You're staying here, as I said, and you're not going to move until I get back, which might not be until daylight."

"Where are you going?"

Dread washed over her. He couldn't simply leave her here. On impulse, Della reached for him again.

"You're safe here, if you do as I say." He turned away. By the sound of his grunt, he'd swung up on the horse's back. "I need to look for my brother. Stay under those trees, and don't leave this spot."

He spoke quietly, but the force behind his words left a greater impact than if he'd shouted at her. Seconds later, he was gone, and the area around her became eerily quiet. An occasional rustling in the underbrush or in the canopies of the trees were the only sounds to keep her company.

Della held her hands in front of her, feeling her way to the trunk of a nearby tree, and sank to the ground. Her body ached and throbbed, and she shivered. She slipped her arms through the large buckskin jacket, and drew her legs up under her skirts.

A million thoughts raced through her mind. What if he didn't come back? What if the Pawnee found him . . . or her? She hadn't even considered that his brother had been with him when he'd been shot.

She closed her eyes, her heart beating wildly in her chest. If she survived through this night, she could survive anything. For now, she had no choice but to do what Matthew Osborne had told her, and remain where she was. She'd figure out what to do later, if he wasn't back by dawn.

Della opened her eyes. She squinted into the bright light.

Birds chirped loudly among the tree branches overhead. She braced her hand to sit up, and connected with the solid feel of another person. Startled, she yanked her hand away and scrambled to put some distance between them.

Matthew Osborne! He'd come back. He lay motionless on his side, his back turned to her. When had he returned?

She darted a hasty glance around. They were in a heavily wooded area. How had he led them to this spot in the darkness the night before? She inched away from him, to maintain a more proper distance, half expecting her father to charge between the trees and tell her she'd committed a sinful act. Her face flamed. How long had he lain next to her? They were close enough for their bodies to touch not a moment ago.

Della dismissed her thoughts. This was the middle of the wilderness. Her father wasn't here to judge her, and nothing inappropriate had happened. She'd saved this man's life yesterday, and he'd surely saved hers. They depended on each other.

Hesitating slightly, she reached her hand out to touch his shoulder. She leaned over him, swiping away some hair from her face that had come loose from her braid. Her cap was long gone. Della nearly laughed. Her father would be livid if he saw her without her head covering, and here she was, in the company of a man, and her hair was exposed.

Matthew Osborne stirred. She pulled her hand away, and straightened. The sheen of moisture on his neck and face in the cool morning air sent a wave of dread through her. Tentatively, she touched the back of her hand to his forehead.

"You're feverish. I told you last night that might happen," she whispered softly, scolding the sleeping man. The fact that she'd been right when he'd accused her of being argumentative several hours ago didn't give her any satisfaction. A fever wasn't a good sign. Pulling out of the hunting jacket, she was about to place it over him, when his eyes opened, and he rolled to his back.

He grimaced, which turned into a forced smile.

"Lying next to you would make any man feverish," he said, his voice giving away his discomfort.

Della scrambled to her feet. She stared, wide-eyed, down at the man. He hadn't been asleep, after all.

"I see you're not right in the mind, either," she stammered, to cover up the rush of heat to her insides at his implication.

His smile widened, and his brown eyes traveled over her, slow and deliberate.

"Maybe."

He groaned when he raised himself to a sitting position. His dark stare met hers. "I brought more willow bark. I'd appreciate it if you'd change my dressing."

Without waiting for an answer, he pulled the many pouches he wore and his shirt over his head. Della stared, then quickly spun around. Until yesterday, when the Indians had ridden into their camp, she'd never seen a fully-grown man's exposed torso before. While the leader who had taken her had worn a buckskin shirt, many of the warriors had worn nothing but leather leggings and breechcloths. She'd been too scared at the time to give them much notice.

"Addy, turn around. You can't tend to my wound with your back to me."

Addy?

She glanced tentatively over her shoulder. He still sat on the ground, his brows raised and staring up at her in amusement. Della turned to face him.

"My name is Adelle Witmer," she said.

He nodded. "Like I said. Addy. It suits you better."

She cocked her head to the side and narrowed her eyes. Other than her sister calling her Della, no one had ever shortened her name to sound like an endearment.

"Mr. Osborne, I don't think--"

"Call me Matthew. No need for formalities out here in the woods."

He reached for one of the pouches he'd pulled from around his neck, and handed it to her. "Please, I'd appreciate it if you'd make a fresh paste and change my dressing. I might just stay alive long enough to get you back to your family."

Della frowned. "This isn't funny. If you hadn't been so stubborn last night, and kept your jacket, you might not be feverish now."

She took the pouch from him, trying to avoid looking at his corded arms, or broad shoulders, or the olive skin of his lean torso that contrasted sharply with the white strip of her petticoat that she'd wrapped around him. Della's mouth went dry.

"A fever is to be expected. The willow bark poultice will keep it from getting worse. I'd sew up the hole in my back, but I don't have a needle, and I can't reach it."

"You need a doctor," she retorted. How could he speak so casually of his wound? Men had died of far lesser injuries.

"I am a doctor." He grinned widely when she gaped at

him. “And I’d appreciate your help so we can leave here, and try and catch up with the wagons.”

Della opened the pouch to avoid having to look at him. What other surprises did this man have in store? One thing was certain. Her chances of getting back to her father and sister were far greater with Matthew Osborne than on her own, or with anyone else.

She ground some of the willow bark into a powder and mixed it with moist dirt and water from the water bladder Matthew handed her, and made a paste like she’d done the night before.

Della unwound the wrapping from Matthew’s torso, forcing her hands to remain steady. He sat with his back to her, giving her a chance to let her eyes wander freely across the planes of his muscles along either side of his spine. Her pulse quickened, and her fingers tingled to touch him. She lifted her hand to the middle of his back, and held it just inches from his skin. He shifted slightly, and she hastily dropped it again.

Della swallowed the growing lump in her throat, and squeezed her eyes shut for a second. Clearing her throat, she refocused her attention on the bandage.

“Your wound is still bleeding a little,” she said when she pulled the wrapping off and the paste fell away.

“Just put the new poultice over it and wrap it again. When we get to a water source, you’ll have to clean it better.”

Della re-tied the bandage around his torso, and breathed a sigh of relief when the task was done. A warm sensation raced through the tips of her fingers from touching him, and her skin flushed even in the cool morning air. She nearly told him to put his shirt on, but that would only make him aware of how his nudity affected her.

"Did you find your brother?" she asked instead.

Della bit down on her lip just as soon as the words were out. Since Matthew had obviously returned alone, was Zach Osborne dead?

"No." His answer came in a low, menacing tone.

Della met his eyes. Pain, sorrow, and a fierce anger, brewed in their depths, and she shuddered slightly. She wouldn't want to get on this man's bad side.

"As soon as I deliver you to the wagons, I'm coming back to find out what happened to him." His voice, deadly calm and quiet, left no doubt that he would do exactly what he said.

"If you didn't have me underfoot, you'd be going after him right now," she surmised. "Were you and your brother coming after me?" she dared to ask the question that had burned in her mind since she'd found him by the river. "I heard gunshots before I escaped."

Matthew stared at her. "I'm getting you to safety first. If my brother is alive, he'll know how to handle himself to make sure he stays alive. If he's dead . . ."

"It's because of me," she whispered, and dropped her gaze to the ground. Silent tears rolled down her face.

A warm, calloused hand reached out and touched her cheek, lifting her face to meet his eyes.

"This isn't your fault." His deep stare tore straight to her soul. "What I really want to know is how you managed to run away." His brows rose, and his lips widened in a forced smile. Della swallowed. His face was so close to hers. He was such a handsome man, rugged, intelligent, kind, and, if needed, fierce and deadly.

"I was left with two guards while the rest of the Indians rode off. When the shots rang out in the distance, one of the men went to investigate. I . . ." She closed her eyes and whispered a quick prayer. "I hit the other man with a rock, and I . . . took his knife, and his horse. I got lost. There was a fork in the stream, and I rode in the wrong direction at first."

Her tears flowed freely now at the memories of yesterday's horrible ordeal. She blinked, and looked at the man who sat so close to her. His smile had widened into a grin, and then he laughed.

"What is so amusing this time?" she said, her words loud and heated.

Matthew pulled her head closer, and he pressed his lips to her forehead. She jerked back in surprise.

"You're an amazing woman, Addy."

"Why? Because I ran? Because I hurt someone?" Her voice rose, and her body trembled with anger.

Matthew's face sobered. "I'm sorry. I know this must have been terrifying for you, and everything you've done has gone against your nature, but you never lost your wit, and you did what you needed to do to survive. You're remarkable."

His tone dropped to a husky whisper with those last words. Della scooted out of his reach. The intensity in his eyes, and in his voice, was too much. What was he doing to her? She was shaken up from all she'd endured and experienced yesterday, and now he was making her feel weak and jumbled up inside with a few simple words and dark stares.

His hand fell away from her cheek. She inhaled deeply to calm her frazzled nerves.

"Will the Pawnee find us?" She asked, trying to steer the conversation in a different direction.

"All but a few left the area. After they attacked Zach and me, it appears as if they split up. Seems like we surprised them as much as they surprised us. They were, no doubt, on the way back to attack the wagons when we interfered with their plans. They must have decided that a few would head back to their village while the rest would go after the wagons. That's why I think Zach might be alive."

Della's eyes widened. "But if they want to attack the wagons, then my sister, and father, and the rest of the men are in danger."

Matthew reached for her arm. "Bridger and Sublette took your father and everyone else to safety. If they made it to the mountains, the Pawnee won't attack. They will be in Lakota territory."

That dark stare locked on hers again. "We'll meet up with the wagons. We'll have to go a different route, and we'll have to be cautious. The Pawnee won't like that you outwitted them."

"I'll do whatever it takes." Della didn't back down from his stare.

His slow smile made her limbs go weak all over again. "I have no doubt you will."

CHAPTER EIGHT

Matthew pulled a short willow stick from one of his pouches, and chewed on the cut end. He needed to brew some tea from the bark, but he couldn't risk starting a fire. There were still Pawnee in the area. He couldn't let on to Addy how much pain he was in, or that his fever had him worried. As much as he wanted to push to catch up with the wagons, he needed a day to recover, or he wouldn't be of any use in getting Addy to safety.

"I don't think you're in any condition to travel." Addy had one hand on her hip. "It's not worth dying due to stubbornness."

Matthew grinned. Having this little slip of a woman glaring down at him reminded him of his mother, whenever she told him what to do. His father had often complained about his wife's fiercely independent streak, and how he had trouble keeping her in line. He'd always said it with a twinkle in his eye, however, and a smile on his face.

Damn, Papa. I think I'm turning into you. I may have found the same kind of woman you did.

It was no secret in the mountains, or to anyone who knew his folks, that his mother had his father completely wrapped around her fingers. They shared a mutual love and respect for each other that he'd rarely seen in other couples back east.

Matthew drowned in Addy's inquisitive eyes. Was that why he'd never let himself get close to another woman before? He wanted what his parents had, and he'd never come across a woman who could give him that?

Until now.

How can you be so sure, Osborne? You still don't know anything about her.

Why had she caught his eye right from the start? She was a survivor. She had grit. Matthew's lips twitched in a smile. Hell. She stood up to him. She wouldn't crumble when faced with danger or hardships. She'd already proven that.

Addy's brows rose in a silent question. She didn't look away when he locked his gaze on hers. Matthew gritted his teeth, and heaved himself off the ground. It was time to stop daydreaming. Time to stop thinking about his overwhelming attraction to this plucky little woman.

Her eyes widened when he stood to his full height. They lingered on his chest for a moment before she raised her head to look up at him. His lips twitched, and an overpowering sensation rushed through him that was both heat, and something that turned every one of his limbs weak.

Beneath the apprehension and slight fear in her eyes, there was also curiosity, determination, and two emotions that heightened those stirrings in him – desire and attraction. While she might be aware of her feelings, she was afraid of them. Judging by how her father treated her and kept her under watch at all times, she'd never been alone in the company of a man, and she was most likely confused.

"I think you're right," he said. "We're safe here for a day. By tomorrow, the Pawnee who were left behind to find you will have given up."

Her forehead wrinkled. She obviously hadn't expected him to agree with her.

"How do you know we're safe here, and that they won't find us?"

"Because right through those trees is the camp from where you escaped yesterday." Matthew turned slightly and pointed to the west.

"What?" Her eyes widened with panic.

"Lower your voice, Addy." Matthew stepped closer and reached for her hand. "Sound carries far through the woods. Those warriors are looking for you along the streams heading west. The last thing they will think is that you've backtracked and stayed in the area. This is the safest place to be."

He gave her hand a slight squeeze, the contact sending renewed awareness through him. Was it just the fever, or was this what the stirrings of love felt like? The willow bark he was chewing on had better start working soon and bring his fever down. There was no telling what he might say to her in his feverish state.

When she tugged her hand away, he let go, even if his instinct was to pull her closer. His jaw muscles twitched. His primary focus right now had to be getting her to safety, not his wayward thoughts about a woman who would, most likely, return to her family once they caught up with the wagons.

Her father doesn't want her back.

Matthew mentally shook his head. Witmer had spoken those words in anger. No father would cast his own daughter away like that. It would have been a convenient way to keep Addy with him, but even though there was attraction in her eyes, she wouldn't choose him over her father and sister.

Matthew turned away from her. He reached for his shirt on the ground, a grimace on his face when he bent forward. He was used to pain. Growing up in the wilderness, he was no stranger to getting hurt and pushing through the discomfort, but his stirrings for this woman somehow magnified all of his body's senses. Her eyes quickly dropped away from him when he faced her again.

"You did a remarkable job covering up your tracks yesterday. About as well as any woodsman."

Matthew concealed his smile, and pulled his shirt over his head. Her shyness was endearing to a point, but it was her curiosity that sent his heart beat up a notch.

"What do you mean?" she asked. "I don't even know how to cover up my tracks."

"Well, then you're born for a life in the wilderness. Keeping your horse in the water, changing course, and riding both banks of a creek or river are effective ways to throw someone off your tracks."

Addy raised her head and gaped at him. "I was lost. I had no idea where to go."

"By now, those Pawnee have got one hell of a dose of respect for you."

He grinned. She frowned in disapproval.

"Sorry," he mumbled for his choice of words. His eyes lingered on her uncovered hair. The auburn strands shimmered like a copper penny in the sunlight. He hadn't seen it uncovered until today, but her disheveled braid hung down her back nearly to her waist, making her even more attractive. A slight shiver of desire rushed through him, aggravating his injury. What would it feel like to run his fingers through her unbound hair?

"What are your plans, Mr. Osborne . . . Matthew?" she asked, averting her gaze. "How will we get back to the wagons?"

Matthew cleared his throat, thankful for her question to rein in his wandering mind. He gathered his pouches and hung them, crisscross, around his neck and shoulders.

"We stay here for today. I don't have my rifle, so I need to make a weapon. Your knife and my ax won't be enough to fend off a possible attack. Tomorrow, we'll head into the Black Hills, and toward the Wind River from there." He paused, and looked at her. "We have to travel on foot. I released the horse last night. It was too risky keeping it."

Addy nodded in quiet acceptance. Matthew took a step closer. The faint scent of soap lingered on her skin, despite the dirt and grime that covered her. It was a scent he'd come to associate with her, after having her so close to him these past hours.

"I'll do everything I can to get you back to your family," he said in a low tone. His hand reached up, and his fingers grazed her soft cheek.

An uneasy smile formed on her lips. "I have faith in you," she whispered. Her soft eyes stared up at him, so full of wonder and apprehension. Matthew leaned forward, just as she stepped out of his reach.

His jaw muscles twitched. He restrained himself from reaching for her again. What would it take to earn her complete trust, to have her come willingly into his arms?

~

Matthew woke with a start. He pushed himself to a sitting position. Sweat covered his face and neck, and he sucked in a hiss at the sharp pain to his back from his quick movement.

"Addy?" he rasped.

He blinked to focus his eyes. Judging by the sun to the west, it was late in the day. How long had he been asleep? All morning, he'd worked on making a bow that would at least give him some kind of weapon other than his ax and the knife Addy had taken from the Pawnee. Proper bow making would take more time than one day, but it gave him something to do while waiting for his fever to subside.

Several hours must have passed since he'd fallen into a fitful sleep. He'd finally given in to Addy's pleas that he close his eyes for a while. Feeling weak and helpless hadn't sat well with him, but she was right. If he was to get better faster, he needed rest. The willow branches he'd chewed on hadn't done their job as effectively to bring his fever down as if he'd had some willow bark tea.

His mother had often said that a fever wasn't always a bad thing, that it was the body's way of fighting off, what she'd called, an infection. As a young boy, he'd fought a raging fever for days when his leg had festered after he'd accidentally cut himself with a blow of an ax to his foot while chopping wood.

His mother hadn't let on at the time, but she'd been worried for his life. She'd told him much later that she'd feared she'd have to amputate his leg. She'd treated him with all the medicines at her disposal, and she'd made him better. All he had at the moment was willow bark. It would have to be enough to fight off any infection and keep his fever down. Addy depended on him to get her back to her family.

Matthew stood. His head was much clearer now, and his fever was gone. Addy had hovered over him like his mother had done, trying to keep him cool and comfortable. The feelings and sensations she aroused in him with her tender woman's touch were anything but motherly. Matthew cursed silently. She was a woman beyond his wildest dreams.

She might not know it, because she'd never been allowed to do anything on her own, or live life the way it was meant to be lived, but she was a survivor. She did the right things without being aware of what she was doing. She might be afraid, but she was fearless.

Matthew frowned. Where had she gone? He couldn't call out to her. It would make too much noise. His eyes scanned their makeshift camp. A strip of her petticoat lay on the ground, still damp from when she'd placed it on his feverish forehead earlier. His water bladder was gone.

Damn. Had she gone to get water? He should have told her not to go to the creek until it was dark. Sudden apprehension filled him. His hand went straight to the tomahawk at his belt, and he headed in the direction of the water. He'd almost reached the creek, when movement through the trees stopped him. Matthew ducked behind a wide trunk. Slowly, he glanced around the tree.

Two Pawnee warriors pointed toward the clearing. They gestured with their hands, leaving no question that they had seen something that excited them. Matthew clenched his jaw. He could take one man down easily with a throw of his ax. How many more warriors were there? His eyes scanned the forest, but there was no other movement.

Taking care not to step on a twig, he moved away from the tree, crouching low to follow the Indians. They had their sights set on something ahead of them, and he stayed a safe distance to their right. The Pawnee were heading straight for the creek. By the time Matthew reached the clearing, he cursed under his breath.

Addy knelt at the creek bank, her back turned to him and the Indians. Off to his left, the two warriors emerged from the trees, heading straight for her. They'd be on her before she even knew what was coming. Apparently, they seemed to feel rather confident that there was no danger to them, since neither of them had strung their bows.

Matthew's eyes darted between Addy and the Indians, calculating the distance, and what he had to do. He stepped into the clearing, aimed, and threw his ax. He gritted his teeth at the pain in his side with the effort, but he didn't stop to wait for his weapon to hit its target. He rushed forward.

Addy called his name, but his focus remained on the man in front of him. One warrior fell to the ground, while the other whipped around to face him. Stunned with surprise, the warrior stood motionless for a fraction of a second before he reacted. Matthew threw himself at the

Indian before he had a chance to reach for an arrow to string his bow. With a heavy thud, he pushed the man to the ground.

Fighting off the blackness that swirled in front of his eyes from the pain in his back when he made impact with the ground, Matthew groped at his opponent. He threw his full weight into the warrior to try and bring him more fully underneath him and press him to the ground. The Pawnee managed to unsheathe his knife, and Matthew grabbed his wrist before the Indian stabbed at him.

Somewhere in the distance, Addy's terrified voice rang in his ears. Were there more warriors? With renewed determination, Matthew gritted his teeth and shut out the pain in his back. He wrapped his right thigh over his opponent's legs, and by sheer force, pushed him onto his back. His right hand clamped firmly around the Pawnee's wrist, keeping the sharp blade away from him. Blinding pain nearly paralyzed his right side where his wound tore through his insides.

The Pawnee bared his teeth, staring up at him with hate-filled eyes. Matthew straddled his foe. His arm trembled from exertion as he forced the man's wrist backward while his other hand pushed down to immobilize the warrior's free arm against his side. The Indian bucked and writhed beneath him, and Matthew nearly lost his grip with his legs. His strength was fading fast. He couldn't hold on any longer to overpower his opponent.

A sudden splash of water hit the Indian's face, sending cold droplets up into Matthew's eyes. The warrior's muscles tensed, then relaxed, no doubt from the unexpected jolt. Matthew seized his chance. He released his grip with his left hand, and sent his fist against the Pawnee's jaw. The man's body went limp instantly.

Matthew sucked in several quick breaths of air, and pried the knife from the warrior's hand. He pushed away from the limp body, and stood on shaky legs. Still catching his breath, he looked to where Addy stood a few feet away, hugging the water bladder to her chest. Wide-eyed, she stared at him.

Matthew's heart pounded against his ribs. His lips widened in a smile. Addy stood immobile for another second, then she rushed forward. She expelled a cry and threw herself at him. Matthew staggered backward a few steps, holding back a curse. Tender warmth in his chest quickly replaced the pain that seared through him. He clamped his arms around the woman who sobbed against his shirt. He closed his eyes, and inhaled a deep breath.

"I'm so sorry," she cried repeatedly.

"It's all right," Matthew murmured into her hair, his own arms trembling while she shook in his embrace. All the pain was worth it just to hold and feel her in his arms.

CHAPTER NINE

Della submersed the water bladder in the fast-flowing creek, and corked it when it was full. Setting it aside, she cupped her hands in the water again, then held them to her lips. The refreshing liquid soothed her parched throat.

After drinking her fill, she glanced up the steep and rocky slope from where the water tumbled. She sat fully on her haunches and pulled her knees up under her skirt. She sighed, and raised her chin to the wind, closing her eyes. The strong scent of sweet grass and meadow flowers filled her nose, and a smile passed over her lips. She held her wet hands, chilled by the water, to her cheeks.

Crickets chirped, and birds sang in the nearby bushes. The tranquility of this place enveloped her in a sense of peace she hadn't felt in quite a while. She dipped her hands in the water again, and dabbed at her cheeks and neck. Despite being tired to near exhaustion, the cool water invigorated her.

Della glanced over her shoulder. Matthew was out of

sight. He'd asked her to wait here by the stream while he went off to scout the area and search for some food. Making a hasty decision, she unbuttoned the top buttons on her dress to expose more of her neck, and cooled her skin with her moist hands.

There was no harm in indulging in the quick refreshment. She untied the piece of string that held her braid together, and unwound her hair. Raking her fingers through it like a brush, she untangled the snarls that had tugged at her scalp for days. One of the first things she would do when they reunited with the wagons was scrub her hair clean. For now, a quick re-braiding would have to do.

After re-tying the ends of the braid with her string, she tilted her head back and gazed up at the dark blue sky. Puffy white clouds drifted lazily above her, and several birds soared overhead. Matthew had called an early halt to their day when they'd come across this gurgling spring a short time ago. She wouldn't have asked to stop yet, but her relief must have been evident on her face.

"You're holding up well," he'd told her in that sultry tone that never failed to send shivers down her spine, those dark eyes staring at her with an admiration that grew in intensity as each day passed. He'd touched a hand to her arm, then dropped it just as quickly, and told her he'd be back shortly.

"Matthew," she whispered his name into the breeze. A slight chill of delight passed through her as she said it, and her body tingled from the inside out. Her eyes drifted over the tall grasses growing along the creek, and she plucked at one of the blades, weaving it between her fingers. She inhaled deeply, and smiled.

Ten days had passed since her escape from the Pawnee, when she'd found Matthew by the river. He'd saved her life the following day when she'd been careless and gone to fetch water. He hadn't been angry with her for leaving the safety of the trees, even though he'd had every right to be. He'd nearly died once already, trying to get her back from the Pawnee, and he'd put his life at risk for her a second time, even as injured as he was.

He'd held her in his arms that day, and she'd never felt more protected and cared for in her life. He was a man who'd lay down his life for her without blinking. She'd been drawn to him since she'd first seen him ride into her father's camp, but at that moment, a deeper emotion had ignited in her. For the first time, the powerful stirrings of a woman's feelings for a man had taken hold in her heart.

She had no other explanation for the way he made her feel. Her heart raced for no clear reason whenever he was near. Her skin and the rest of her came alive with a simple glance directed at her. Della blinked back the sudden tears in her eyes. All her life, she'd been told by her father that such feelings only led to sinful behavior.

She shook her head. How she wished she had a woman to talk to. How could such feelings be wrong? She'd grown up without a mother for the last ten of her twenty years. She couldn't recall her parents ever laughing or sharing a tender moment. When she'd embraced Matthew that day, and when he'd held her, it was already more than she'd ever seen her parents do. Nothing had ever felt more right.

After she'd stepped out of his comforting embrace that day, Della had immediately noticed the blood soaking through his shirt. His wound had started to bleed again, and she'd had to tear more of her petticoats to bandage him up. Matthew had tied up both of the Pawnee while they were still unconscious, and taken their weapons. He'd told her they would travel through the night to put some distance between them and the Indians. He'd been convinced that the warriors wouldn't follow them again once they freed themselves.

For the next ten days, Matthew had led her through deep gullies and washes, over steep hills, and through thick forests. He'd pushed forward relentlessly, and turned a deaf ear whenever she'd protested that he needed to rest and heal. He'd provided food and shelter, and a warm fire for her each night.

His wound had stopped bleeding by the third day, and she'd continued to wrap it with poultices made of various plants he'd found and deemed suitable along the way. Each day, he'd encouraged her to keep going when exhaustion had taken hold in her. Her feet were sore and blistered, but she didn't complain. His looks of admiration and pride, his words of praise, or when he touched her in some way when she needed assistance navigating a particularly rough stretch of terrain, fueled her desire to please him. His actions also served to nurture her growing feelings for this man.

Guilt consumed her for thinking about how nice it had felt to be held in his arms that day by the stream, and for wishing that he'd do it again. She'd convinced herself that he'd only done it to console her because she'd been distraught. She'd been the one who'd rushed into his arms, after all. Perhaps those intense stares didn't mean what she wanted to believe – that Matthew harbored feelings for her, too. Her father's voice echoed in her mind, telling her that she ought to be ashamed of herself for her wayward thoughts about a man.

The sound of a faint cry startled her from her daydreams. Della's eyes snapped open, and she sat up straighter. Had she imagined a little child's cry? She cocked her head to the side. No. There it was again. She scrambled to her feet, her eyes scanning along the trees that marked the beginning of the forest. The cries came again, a little louder this time. Della splashed through the creek, and followed the sound. She hadn't gone more than a few steps into the thicket, when she nearly stepped on a dark-haired child, no older than two years. The little boy stared up at her, his dark skin covered in streaks of dirt and tears.

Della shot a nervous glance over her shoulder and around her. Where were this child's parents? The forest was thick with undergrowth and greenery, which completely hid this boy from view.

Della dropped to her knees. "I won't hurt you," she whispered softly, and reached out her hand. The toddler came to her, and Della scooped him into her arms.

"Where did you come from?" she asked. "Where's your mama?"

The little boy, dressed in a leather shirt that fell past his knees, sobbed against her shoulder. She pushed her sudden apprehension aside. If there was an Indian child here, there would be adults nearby, as well. Had this baby wandered away from his family, and gotten lost? Surely no one would have abandoned him.

She carried the child from the dense bushes and back to the creek. Setting him by the water, she offered him a drink from the water bladder, and washed his face. She didn't have any food to give him, but he seemed content to rest in her arms at the moment. She'd wait for Matthew to return to see what to do about this boy.

Della hummed a quiet tune, and rocked the baby in her arms. His sobs had stopped, and he was nearly asleep. Twigs snapped loudly over the sounds of the gurgling water. Della turned her head toward the sound.

"Matthew?" she called, and scrambled to her feet, holding the toddler in her arms.

Relief flooded her when he emerged from a different part of the forest. Her smile faded when two men dressed in nothing but loincloths followed him. She held the baby close, and waited.

A surprised look passed over the men's faces. The two Indians talked excitedly, and one rushed forward. Della hugged the little boy to her, her eyes darting from the Indian to Matthew, who looked just as surprised as the Indians. He moved toward her.

"Addy, these men have been looking for that child."

Della hesitated, then handed the baby to the Indian who'd rushed to her. He nodded at her, a grateful look in his eyes. She returned the gesture, and smiled at him.

"I found this baby in the bushes," she said when Matthew reached her side.

"He wandered away from his family a while ago. His parents have looked everywhere. I ran into them a short distance from their village."

"Village?" Della frowned. There was an Indian village nearby? She pushed aside her momentary sensation of dread.

"These are Lakota. They're friendly," Matthew said, as if he'd read her mind.

The father of the child spoke to Matthew, and gestured with his hands into the distance. He looked at Della, and nodded at her.

"Looks like we're invited to the village." Matthew grinned. "This man is the son of Chief Running Bear, and he wants to express his thanks to you for finding his son by offering us a meal and a place to sleep tonight."

Della hesitated. Her last encounter with Indians hadn't been cordial.

Matthew leaned toward her. "They're friendly," he repeated in a reassuring tone. "And very hospitable. I've stayed with bands of Lakota before during my travels."

Della nodded. "All right," she whispered. She trusted Matthew, and if he believed these Indians were friendly, she had no cause to doubt him.

Matthew took hold of her hand, and nodded at the Indian, who waited with an expectant look in his eyes. Della hurried to keep up with his long strides when he led her away from the stream to follow the men. His hand swallowed up her smaller one, and the further through the forest they moved, the firmer his grip became. When they entered a large clearing, and more than a dozen Indian tipis came into view, Matthew pulled her up so close to him that her hip bumped his thigh. Della darted a quick look up at him. When their eyes connected, the breath left her lungs. A tender, yet possessive gleam flashed in his gaze.

The people of the village greeted them and the two men with friendly smiles and curious stares. Women stopped what they were doing in front of their tipis, children ran up to them, and men stood, watching. One woman in particular came running at them, and the man carrying the toddler handed the boy to her. The two exchanged words and the woman looked toward Della. She nodded vigorously, and smiled. Della returned the gesture.

Matthew finally released her hand when he greeted and conversed with an older man who'd emerged from the largest tipi in the middle of the village. Della rubbed her fingers against her sweaty palm, which still tingled from his touch. She stood silently beside him while the Indian and he spoke in words and hand gestures that made no sense to her. A few times, Matthew glanced at her, or motioned to her, and the old man nodded and smiled in apparent approval.

Finally, Matthew turned to her. "Chief Running Bear is honored to have us here as his guests. I've told him about the Pawnee attack, and how you escaped from them. He wants to honor your bravery, and show his appreciation for finding his grandson by giving us food and shelter for the night."

Della's eyes widened. "Honor my bravery?"

Matthew grinned. "When someone outwits their enemies, it's definitely something to celebrate. And, on top of that, you found his grandson." His face sobered, but genuine relief swept through his eyes. "He also told me that Zach is alive. This village heard about what happened from another village. They apparently took in a white man who escaped from a war party of Pawnee."

Della smiled. Impulsively, she put her hand on his arm. "Matthew, that's wonderful news."

He returned her smile. "Yeah, it is," he said, his voice deepening. He swayed slightly toward her, or had she simply imagined it? Abruptly, he straightened, and laughed. "He was obviously in a hurry to get home. The chief said he'd already left to head for the Wind River Range, even though they offered to keep him until he regained all his strength."

"It doesn't surprise me that he didn't take their advice, if he's anything like you."

Matthew's eyes darkened, and his lips twitched. Relief flooded Della that his brother was safe. She couldn't imagine the pain of losing her own sister.

"We'll meet up with him once we get to the rendezvous site."

The old Indian chief laughed heartily, and spoke again. Della tore her eyes away from Matthew. The chief pointed at her, then at Matthew. Matthew laughed at whatever the man had said.

"Running Bear said his wife and daughter-in-law will take you to get cleaned up. He thinks we both look travel weary." He grinned. "It's his polite way of saying we smell bad and look worse."

Della's heart skipped a beat with dread. "What about you? I don't understand their language. Can't I stay with you?"

Matthew chuckled. He leaned toward her, his breath against her cheek sending shivers up her spine. "You don't want me there, Addy. I'm sure you've wanted a full bath for weeks, if not longer. The women will take you to where you can clean up, in private." He took a step back, his eyes lingering on her face. "I'm going to have the medicine man take a look at my wound."

Della hesitated, then nodded. She raised her chin. She was behaving like a scared little mouse, and for no apparent reason. "You're right. Getting clean does sound wonderful. I'm sure I'm wearing an inch of dirt at least."

An older woman appeared from inside the tipi, and spoke to the chief. She smiled warmly at Della, who returned the gesture. The woman reached for her elbow, and motioned with her hand. She spoke, and Della looked to Matthew.

"Go with her," he said.

Della allowed the woman to lead her away, through the village toward the edges of the trees, where dense bushes lined a wide, slow-moving stream that looked fairly deep. She turned her head to look for Matthew one final time, but she didn't see him.

The woman Della recognized as the little boy's mother met them by the stream. She carried a large basket at her hip, and smiled warmly. She appeared to be no older than herself. Della blinked in surprise when she and the older woman began to strip out of their doeskin clothes. Her eyes widened, and she quickly turned her back. Behind her, the old woman cackled. A bony hand touched her arm, and Della turned. She focused on the woman's face, rather than her complete nudity. The woman spoke, gesturing at Della's dress. Her meaning became clear.

Della glanced up, toward the village, and along the banks of the stream. Only the tops of the tipis were visible, and the thin wisps of smoke that rose into the sky from the fires. Her lips tightened in a firm line, and she looked toward the water again. Her skin itched. Inhaling a deep breath, she cast her inhibitions aside and reached for the buttons on her dress.

CHAPTER TEN

The sun was slowly sinking into the western horizon. Della ran the brush fashioned from porcupine quills through her hair a final time, and smiled at the two Indian women. Her initial inhibitions had quickly vanished after she'd followed the women into the stream. Although the water hadn't been warm, washing away many weeks of accumulated grime felt like heaven. The last time she'd indulged in a full wash had been at Fort Williams, and even then, she'd had to use a small tub she'd barely fit in.

Her skin tingled all over from scrubbing it with some roots the women had given her, and shown her how to use. She'd even used the lather created by the roots to wash her hair.

The old woman croaked a few words, and patted Della's hand. Della handed the brush back to her, and reached for her wet dress. It would have to dry overnight before she could wear it again, but it had needed a good washing. The soft doeskin dress she wore in the meantime reached just past her ankles. The rest of her legs were wrapped in soft hide, and her blistered feet found relief in the comfortable leather moccasins the mother of the toddler had urged her to put on. No wonder Matthew wore moccasins in favor of boots.

Della followed the women away from their secluded bathing area. They returned to the village, stopping in front of one of the outlying tipis. The younger woman lifted the flap to the opening, and motioned for Della to enter.

"Thank you, for everything." Della smiled, and clasped the old woman's hands.

Would Matthew come and see her, or had he gone to be with the men? Della's eyes traveled through the village, but his familiar figure was nowhere to be seen.

Both women smiled brightly, nodded, then turned and walked away. Della ducked into the dim interior of the dwelling. How wonderful it would be to not sleep out in the open for just one night. Her mouth watered at the smell of food coming from within. The shadows of a fire danced on the hides that made up the walls. She adjusted her eyes to the light, and froze. A man wearing some sort of headdress with feathers and buffalo horns knelt beside another man lying on a pile of furs.

"Matthew?"

Della's eyes widened. Her heart nearly dropped to her stomach. Matthew was nude from the waist up, lying on his stomach. The Indian with the headdress glanced over his shoulder, then stood. He ignored Della as he moved past her and left the tipi. Matthew rolled to his side, and slowly stood. She lifted her eyes to meet his stare from across the space within the tipi, and her mouth went dry.

"Addy," he said, his husky voice holding a hint of surprise.

Della's pulse quickened. His gaze slowly traveled up and down her body, and he moved around the fire toward her. He drew her in with his stare when he stopped directly in front of her.

"You clean up nice," he said. The flames from the fire danced in his dark eyes as he looked down at her. When his calloused hands reached for hers, Della sucked in a quick breath. He stood so close, the clean scent of his skin was intoxicating. She'd gotten used to looking at his nude chest, back, and arms during their time together over the last ten days, but her face flamed in reaction to seeing him now.

Why did it feel so different this time? He'd only removed his shirt whenever she treated his wound. By the looks of the leather band around his abdomen, someone had already done that.

"I didn't think you'd be here," she stammered. Her heart beat up into her throat. "We'll be sharing this tent? Alone?" Her voice was weak and foreign-sounding in her own ears.

Matthew chuckled. "We've been alone together for nearly two weeks, and it hasn't bothered you."

Della's gaze dropped to the fur pallets on the ground, then back to the man who made her feel things, made her want things, that she'd been told were wrong and sinful.

"Yes, but, this is different."

"How is this different, Addy?" There was an almost angry note to his voice. "Have I done anything inappropriate, or given you a reason to be afraid of me?" He let go of her, and turned away. He ran a hand through his hair.

She quickly shook her head. "No, you haven't."

Matthew stood with his back to her, his muscles tense and rigid. When he finally faced her again, the anger had vanished, replaced by a roguish smile. "I hope you don't decide to stay and become a Lakota woman."

Della tilted her head to her side. "Why would I do that?"

"You look real nice in that dress." His voice had gone husky. He closed the distance between them in one stride.

"I'm only wearing it while my dress dries. It needed a good washing." His compliment sent a surge of warmth through her, and gave her the courage to ease the tension between them. She raised her chin, and mimicked his smile. "My father wouldn't approve."

Matthew stared at her, then laughed. "Your father isn't here."

"No, he's not. I prefer my own clothing for when we leave here, but it has nothing to do with my father."

Matthew's eyes roamed her face, lingered on her unbound hair, then locked on her eyes. "You're beautiful no matter what you wear."

Della's knees weakened at his unexpected words. Heat started in the middle of her chest and traveled outward. Words refused to come. She stood rooted to the spot when Matthew whispered her name. He bent forward, his breath on her face. He hesitated, then touched his lips to hers.

Della's breath caught in her throat at his startling action. Her heart must have stopped beating. The instant his mouth was on hers, new sensations she'd never experienced exploded inside her. She leaned toward him, shutting out her father's voice that her behavior was bad. Matthew's arms wrapped around her middle, and he pulled her up against him. Della leaned into the strength of his embrace without hesitation. Her arms snaked up and around his neck of their own will, her fingers exploring along the smooth contours of his skin.

A low groan rumbled in Matthew's chest. He covered her mouth more fully with his, and moved his lips across hers. Della's mind swirled, until she no longer formed a conscious thought. There was only Matthew, and the burning need he brought to life in her. His hands stroked up and down her back, his fingers weaving through her hair, until his actions slowed, and he eased his mouth away from hers.

Della opened her eyes to stare up at the man who held her with such tender strength, that she could do nothing but lean into him. Her chest heaved as she tried to catch her breath.

"I've wanted to do that since the first time I saw you," he rasped. His hand stroked along her cheek, pushing her hair from her face. "I can see it in your eyes that you're thinking the same thing."

She shook her head to deny what he said. She'd be lying if she spoke the words.

"Don't be afraid of what's happening, Addy. Don't be afraid of me."

"I could never be afraid of you," she whispered. "I don't know what's happening to me. All I know is that I have thoughts and feelings about you that I've never had for anyone else. When you look at me, and . . . when you touch me, I don't want the feelings to stop." Della groped for the right words to tell him what she meant. She gazed up into his smoldering eyes, and all doubt vanished. "My father would definitely not approve of my behavior," she added with a sly smile.

Matthew's brows rose in astonishment at her words. Once again, she'd surprised him, just as her reaction to his kiss had surprised him. He certainly hadn't planned on kissing her this evening. No doubt he'd wanted to. It had gotten more difficult each day not to, but when she'd come into that tipi, all cleaned up and with her hair unbound, he hadn't been able to stop himself. He laughed.

"Then it's definitely a good thing that your father's not here," he murmured. He dipped his head again, and touched his lips to hers. Addy stiffened slightly in his arms, which stopped him from repeating his actions from a moment ago. He drew back, studying her eyes. The wonder, the confusion, and the desire shimmering in her brown depths caused sensations and reactions in him that he fought to keep under control. He needed to tread lightly, or he'd scare her away. This was new to her, and she needed time to sort through her feelings.

He'd lain awake nearly every night, aching to hold her like he was holding her now. Instead of following his desires, he'd slept on the other side of their campfire, glad for the cold nights to temper his simmering body.

The way she molded herself to him now was as if she was made for him alone. Matthew closed his eyes and inhaled deeply of the clean scent of her skin and hair. She was here willingly, not out of fear after a frightening experience with the Pawnee.

A fierce possessiveness came over him, just like it had that day he fought off the warriors by the stream. He could have easily killed both warriors. His ax had stopped the first one, knocking him unconscious, and his fist had done the same to the other. He'd opted to simply tie them up and leave them where he'd defeated them, and taken their weapons. He'd never been one to count coup on another man, but defeating an enemy and allowing him to live would impress the rest of the Pawnee more than if he had killed them. He'd sent a clear message that he was not someone to take on again, that he would defend his woman with his life, and he would win.

He chuckled. He doubted either one of the warriors would admit that a little woman had gotten the better of one of them, and with nothing but a splash of water. Had Addy not intervened when he wrestled with that warrior, Matthew conceded that the outcome of the fight might have been different. It was at that moment, when she'd rushed into his arms after helping him defeat the Indian, that his heart had been hopelessly lost.

While he'd thought he might be falling in love with Addy before, he'd been absolutely sure at that moment. Her quick thinking, her spirit, and her independent nature drew him to her as much, if not more, than her soft beauty. While she was resourceful and confident, her inhibitions -- and what he'd even describe as fear – about her feelings for him, had kept him from acting on his own feelings.

It was obvious in her discreet glances that she was drawn to him as a man. Also obvious was her nervousness around him. Judging by everything he'd seen and heard from her father, she'd been fed a bunch of strict rules and lies about men and women. While he'd grown up watching his parents openly express their love for each other, it wouldn't surprise him if Addy had been told that displays of affection were wrong and perhaps even sinful.

Matthew fought his need to pull her closer, to kiss her again the way he'd done a moment ago. It was too soon to tell her he loved her. She needed time to sort out her feelings. If he told her now, she might turn tail and run. Her father's strict upbringing had ingrained things in her mind, and until she was ready to break those ties, he had to bide his time. Once she understood her own feelings, she could be rid of her father's rigid beliefs. She'd already broken free of him in bits and pieces on her own. It was only a matter of time before she let go completely, but it had to be on her terms.

In the meantime, he'd show her slowly what love could be like between a man and woman. He could be selfish, and tell her what her father had said, that he considered her ruined and didn't want her anymore. Matthew could never subject her to that kind of pain. It would be too easy to bind her to him if he told her. She'd stay with him only because she'd have no other options, not because she'd chosen him.

No. He would never do that to her. Witmer had spoken out of anger. The man would have had second thoughts by now about what he'd said. Once they caught up with the wagons, if Addy wanted to remain with her family, he'd have to let her go.

Matthew drew away from the sweet woman in his arms. He offered a reassuring smile to ease her confusion.

The back of his hand touched her soft cheek. He slid his other arm out from around her waist, and gave her hands a light squeeze.

"How about some food, and then a good night's rest? If we get an early start tomorrow, we can be at the rendezvous site within a week."

CHAPTER ELEVEN

Dozens of thin columns of smoke rose in the air in the distance. A veil of hazy mist hovered just above the tree line in the valley below. The morning had started with gray skies, and the sun was trying to poke through the thick clouds. They'd been close to the site of the rendezvous when they'd stopped to make camp the night before, but Addy had been tired. She'd agreed that morning would be soon enough to catch up with the wagons.

"Looks like we've arrived."

Matthew pointed toward the haze with the hunting bow he'd taken from his Pawnee opponent over three weeks ago. The Wind River Mountain Range stretched out around them, covered in dark forest as far as the eye could see.

Addy pulled the Indian pony she rode to a stop beside him. Her eyes followed to where he pointed, then she turned her head to look at him. An uneasy smile passed over her lips. Matthew moved his horse closer to hers and reached for her hand. She didn't pull away.

"Your father and sister will be glad to see you."

She didn't say anything, and looked off into the distance again. It wasn't what he wanted to say to her. Although it was a relief to finally arrive at their destination, dread consumed him. This might be his final day with Addy. He hadn't planned on staying at rendezvous for long. If Zach was here, he'd be anxious to get home.

The horses the Lakota chief had gifted them had cut their travel time to get to the Wind River down to just over a week. It hadn't been enough time to solidify his fragile relationship with Addy. Over the days that followed their departure from the Lakota village, she'd been more relaxed around him, but she hadn't said a word about their kiss in the tipi.

She'd openly admitted that she had feelings for him that night, but also that they confused her. He hadn't kissed her again for those very reasons. It was better to abstain, for his own sanity. He might not have been able to stop with just a kiss, and Addy wasn't the kind of woman he could simply take to his blankets without the benefit of marriage. Even if she gave herself to him, she'd regret it later, and he'd never dishonor her in such a way.

He'd been trying his hardest to court her like a man would court a woman in the east, and build a foundation for a relationship. It had been one of the hardest things he'd ever endured. Her quick smiles sent his heart to racing, but he never went further than a touch to her arm, or taking hold of her hand whenever the opportunity arose. She'd even been agreeable to sleeping on the same side of the fire each night since they'd left the village, but she'd wrapped herself in the buffalo robe Running Bear had given her like a protective cocoon.

A cordial friendship had formed between them, and she'd laughed at, and eagerly listened to, his stories of his family and growing up in the wilderness. He'd told her of his mother, and how she was a knowledgeable healer, and how he'd wanted to follow in her footsteps and become a doctor. She'd asked him about his time in Boston, and told him of her dull life in New York. As he'd suspected, her father had kept a tight rein on her and her sister, especially after Addy's mother had died.

Matthew's respect for her character had grown stronger each day. Her resilience all these weeks had only strengthened his love for her. Inside, she had to be afraid of everything she'd endured. This was a life he was accustomed to, but to her, it was new and terrifying. Rather than crumbling to pieces, she gained more strength with each experience.

"I can't wait to see my sister," Addy said eagerly. She laughed. "I'm sure she and my father will be surprised that I'm alive."

"Well then, let's not keep them waiting."

Matthew released her hand and nudged his horse in the side. His mood darkened with each step his mount took that would bring him closer to her family, and perhaps losing the woman who occupied his every thought of now and his future. This would have been a good time to bring up that he loved her, but the way she'd talked about missing her sister, and her eagerness to see Mary and her father again, held him back.

"Do you still think I'd be too weak to see the place where you grew up?"

Matthew slowed his horse and waited for her to ride up alongside him. Her question caught him off guard. He groaned silently when she smiled brightly at him, her eyes sparkling with mischief.

"No, I don't," he said curtly. "I think you'd do just fine," he added. What did it matter? She might not ever see the Yellowstone area. She was eager to reunite with her family, and that meant that she'd be continuing west with them. "I don't think your father is going by way of the Yellowstone if he's heading to the Washington Territory."

Addy's smile faded, and she stared at him. Matthew cursed silently for the hurt he'd put in her in her eyes with his gruff remark.

"Let's get to camp," he mumbled, and forced a smile. "I'm eager to find Zach."

Addy followed him in silence, and guilt nagged him for his harsh words and foul mood. Once they found her father and sister, he'd talk to her, and tell her that he loved her. There was still a slight chance that Witmer had meant what he said about not wanting her back. Hopefully it wouldn't come to that. He wanted Addy to make her choice freely, not because she might be forced into something she didn't want to do, not to mention the pain it would cause her.

Laughter, loud voices, and gunshots reached them long before dozens of tents, lean-to's and tipis came into view. Hundreds of trappers, Indians, and even several wagons with traders of all sorts of goods milled about the large open area. Matthew kept a look-out for his comrades. Men he hadn't seen in years called out a greeting, others stared at him and Addy with interest.

"Stay close," he said when he caught the look of astonishment on Addy's face as they passed men who wrestled each other to the ground, knives drawn.

"Isn't anyone going to stop them from killing each other?" she whispered.

"Most everyone here is drunk. I doubt anyone's going to die. This is what goes on at these gatherings. Men drink, carouse, and trade their furs. No one would think to break up one of these fights."

"Barbarians," Addy hissed. She shot him a disapproving frown when he chuckled at her comment.

"Osborne! Matthew Osborne."

Matthew's head turned at the sound of the familiar voice. Jim Bridger rushed around a group of men inspecting a cache of furs. Matthew dismounted his horse, and held out his hand in greeting. The trapper shook it. He cocked his head to the side and looked at him suspiciously.

"It's Matthew, ain't it?" he asked, uncertainty in his voice.

Matthew laughed. "Yeah, Bridger, it's Matthew."

"I'll be," the woodsman said with a loud laugh, and slapped his hand against his thigh. "We thought you was dead."

"No, just took me a little longer to get here." He turned to look at Addy, who still sat on her horse. "I brought Miss Witmer back. Where are my brother and her father?"

Bridger's eyes widened in surprise. "Zach done told us ya was kilt by them Pawnee. He rode through here about a week ago. Said he was headin' home to break the news to yer folks." He glanced toward Addy. "Had us a skirmish with them bloodthirsty Injuns ourselves. Couple of the missionaries got kilt, and a few got hurt, but the rest of us kept our scalps."

Addy gasped at Jim Bridger's words.

"Not your father," Bridger said quickly. He pointed toward the west of the large encampment. "He's camped yonder with his wagons, past them tipis."

Matthew mounted his horse. "Thanks for getting them here safe." He nodded to Bridger.

"Come back and visit with Fitzpatrick an' me fer a spell when you're done with Witmer," Bridger called.

"I will, but I'll be heading out soon. I need to get home and let my folks know that I'm not dead."

Bridger laughed. "Good idea. Ain't every day a man comes back from gettin' kilt."

Matthew led Addy through the throng of men and animals until a group of seven wagons came into view at the edge of camp. He was about to open his mouth to speak, and tell her he needed to talk to her before she saw her father, when she kicked her horse forward toward the wagons.

"Mary," she called.

A girl stood by one of the wagons, securing a rope to the side. A man was hitching mules to the rig next to hers. She looked up, and her hands shot to her mouth. Addy pulled her horse to a stop in front of the girl, and slid from the animal's back. The two embraced, and sobbed loudly.

Matthew guided his horse toward them. Dammit. Now he'd have to wait. Why had he been such a mule's ass and not told her at daybreak that he didn't want to lose her? Or yesterday? Or two days ago?

Isaac Witmer appeared from behind one of the

wagons. He stopped. His eyes widened in disbelief. Addy pulled from her sister's arms, and faced her father.

"Hello, Father," she said. She didn't make a move to embrace him.

The man nodded stiffly. "Adelle," he said, and his eyes drifted to Matthew.

Matthew dismounted his horse, and approached Isaac Witmer. "I told you I'd bring her back. I made good on my word."

Witmer stared, silently, from him to Addy. Finally, he nodded, and addressed his daughter. "You'll find your clothes in the wagon where you left them. Cover your hair and make yourself decent, and prepare to travel." He turned to Matthew. "I prayed you'd bring her back. Forgive my shock at the moment. I was led to believe you were dead."

"He saved my life, Father," Addy said quickly, her eyes going to Matthew.

Witmer's head snapped to her. "And I'm grateful for it." He held out his hand to Matthew. "Thank you," he said. "You've come back just in time. We are preparing to leave shortly."

Matthew shook the man's hand. His heart sank to his gut. He'd run out of time. His eyes drifted to Addy, who'd embraced her sister again. Tears of joy rolled down her cheeks. Despite everything, relief hit him. Isaac Witmer was still the same callous character he remembered, but at least he hadn't rejected his daughter.

He stepped up to her. "Addy, I need to talk to you."

She pulled out of her sister's embrace a second time, and faced him. She shot a hasty glance at her father before her eyes met his.

"I should have said this sooner, but--"

"Osborne? Where the hell are ya? Osborne?"

Matthew cursed under his breath, and turned to the loud and frantic voice of Jim Bridger. A horse charged toward the missionary camp, and came to a skidding halt a few feet in front of him.

"What is the meaning of this?" Isaac Witmer huffed.

Bridger jumped from his horse, ignoring the man. "Ya gotta come quick, Matthew. It's Fitzpatrick. He got in a scuffle with some ornery fella with an eyepatch, and took a bullet. Damn coward hightailed it outta here before we could catch him. We ain't got your ma here this year to do the doctorin', so you gotta come."

Matthew glanced from Bridger to Addy. He ground his teeth. Thomas Fitzpatrick was a good man and long-time friend of his family. He reached for Addy's hand. Silently, he cursed Bridger's timing.

"Don't leave," he said in a low tone. He tore his eyes away from her, and mounted his horse. He kicked the animal into a run, back toward the camp where he'd met up with Bridger. Hopefully, Fitzpatrick's wound wasn't extensive. If Witmer planned to leave, time had run out, and Matthew cursed himself for being a stupid fool for not telling the woman he loved sooner that she belonged with him.

CHAPTER TWELVE

Della stared after him. Matthew had been sullen all morning, and somehow she was the cause of it. The closer they'd come to the rendezvous site, the more closed-off he had become. All week, she'd been hoping – wishing – that he'd kiss her again the way he'd done at the Indian village. A few times, she'd thought about bringing up the subject, but she had no idea how to even start such a conversation.

The more time she spent with him, the stronger her feelings grew. It wasn't simply her attraction to him as a man. He made her laugh, he treated her with kindness and respect, and as an equal. He made her feel safe, and he'd become the best friend she'd ever had.

She'd taken his advice and not been afraid of those feelings, of what was happening to her, but she had no idea how to bring it up with him in conversation. So she'd waited. What would happen now? Her father was ready to leave the rendezvous. Matthew had asked her not to leave, but what had he meant by that? That he wanted to tell her a proper good-bye after all the weeks they'd spent together?

She'd asked him earlier if he still thought that she was too weak to see the wilderness that he called home, hoping he would ask her to go with him. She hadn't expected his gruff reply that her father wouldn't be going there. She didn't want to go with her father. She wanted to go with Matthew, but he hadn't said a word to her that he would like to take her with him.

Della shook her head. She couldn't continue to be in a man's company unless he was her husband. The last few weeks had been out of necessity. Matthew had given no indication that he'd ask for her hand in marriage.

"Have you lain with him?"

Della's head whipped around. Her mouth gaped open, and she stared at her father. Next to her, her sister gasped.

"Have I . . . what?" She shook her head. "How can you even ask me that?" Anger such as she'd never experienced surged through her. She'd barely returned, and her father was suggesting that she'd been with a man without benefit of marriage?

The man who stood before her, her father, stared back at her. "But it's what you want to do. It's what he wants to do." His voice rose, and his face turned red. Something close to disdain filled his eyes. "Look at you. Your hair is as wild and unkempt as an Indian's. You're even dressed like one. There's no telling what you have done to bring shame upon yourself."

Della blinked. Had her father taken leave of his senses? She gritted her teeth. "I did what I had to in order to survive, Father." She moved her toes in the comfortable moccasins she wore. She'd given back the doeskin dress in favor of her simple homespun gown, but couldn't refuse the footwear. Her boots had holes in the bottoms, and left her feet blistered to where she couldn't have walked anymore.

"So you admit that you've lain with him." Her father stepped toward her, pointing a finger at her. If he struck her in the face, it wouldn't be a surprise.

"I admit no such thing," Della shouted, holding her ground. "I haven't lain with any man. Why do you make such accusations?" She ground her teeth, and continued, "Just because I have not had you watching over me, does not mean I don't understand what is proper. I'm a grown woman and able to think for myself."

She leaned toward him, her anger making her bold. She raised her chin and glared at her father. She'd never raised her voice or spoken to him like this before. "What have I done to make you hate me so much, Father?"

Della's hands shook, and tears pooled in her eyes. Her father's brows furrowed, and he backed away from her. "Hate you?" he echoed, his voice dropping to a near whisper.

Della took a step toward him. Her eyes narrowed. "For years, you've treated me as if I was constantly doing something wrong, when all I've done is what you've asked of me. You've disallowed me my freedom to choose the people with whom I associate, and I'm always reminded of my bad behavior, even though I've never done anything against your wishes."

Della's tears flowed freely now, and she swiped a hand at her face. Mary tentatively touched her arm. Della gave her a quick smile, then turned her attention back to her father. He stood, uncharacteristically silent, in front of her, looking at her as if he hadn't seen her before. Della stepped up closer, and stared him in the eyes. His demeanor transformed right in front of her, and he looked years older all of a sudden. Della reached out her hand and placed it on his chest.

She took in a breath to calm herself, then said in a quiet tone, "I've always loved and respected you, Father."

The air left her lungs when he suddenly pulled her into a tight embrace. She stood stiffly, her eyes wide as he pressed her up to him.

"Forgive me," he whispered. "Forgive a father for his sins and wrongdoings. I've never wanted anything but to keep you safe. You are so much like your mother. I thought I'd lost you, like I lost her."

Della pulled out of his embrace. Her forehead wrinkled when she stared up into her father's face. He thought she was like her mother? From what she recalled, her mother had been quiet and meek, which was not how she would describe herself.

Her father held her at arm's length. "You look so much like her. I was taken with her the minute I first saw her, and I asked her father for her hand in marriage. She didn't want to marry me, but neither I nor her father gave her a choice." He stopped, and took in a deep breath. He smiled uneasily. Years of regret flashed in his eyes.

"I forced her into a marriage she didn't want. I thought I could bend her to my will, make her love me, but all I did was push her away. She was an obedient wife, but I never owned her heart. She closed herself off from the world, because of what I had done to her. I took away her friends and her happiness to bind her to me. I see now that I'm doing the same to you. Like you, she asked me why I hated her." He sobbed. "All I did was love her."

He released her, and ran a shaky hand across his face. Della touched his arm. Her father's shocking admission held her rooted to the spot. She hesitated, then leaned against him. "I love you, Father," she whispered.

His chest heaved, and his arms went around her again. "I love you, Adelle," he rasped. "When those Indians took you, I thought I was being punished for making the same mistake with you as I'd made with your mother. You've been a good daughter, and I've done wrong by you. I won't keep you from your happiness." He clasped her arms, and held her away from him. He smiled. "Follow your heart."

Della cocked her head. "Follow my heart?"

Her father nodded. "I've decided to abandon my mission. Some trappers have agreed to guide us back to Fort Williams, and from there, to the Missouri. I'm heading back to New York, and I will resume my ministry there." He looked to where Mary had stood quietly off to the side. "When those Indians took you, I nearly went mad. I thought I'd lost one daughter because of my stupidity. I won't put Mary in danger." His grip on Della's arms tightened. "I won't stop you if you choose not to go with us."

Della's eyes widened. What was he saying? Her father gave her a quick shake. "Your heart is with Matthew Osborne, girl. He loves you. I've seen it in his eyes. If you love him, go to him. You have my blessing."

She blinked at this sudden turn of events. Slowly, she nodded. She loved Matthew. She'd known it for weeks, but she'd been too scared to tell him. Her heart pounded in her chest as her father's words sank in, and because of everything she'd just learned. Her father, always so rigid and unapproachable, had laid out his soul to her. He wanted her to be happy, and follow her heart. There was only one place she wanted to be.

"I have to talk to him," she whispered. Was her father correct, and Matthew loved her, too?

Don't be afraid of what's happening.

Her father released her. Della gave her sister a quick hug, then she turned and ran through the large camp, dodging the throng of trappers, mountain men, and Indians. She ignored the rude calls from some of the men, and ran as if a war party of Pawnee was on her heels. She darted among men, horses, and tipis until she reached the place where Jim Bridger had stopped them earlier. Her chest heaved, and she fought to catch her breath.

"Can I interest ya in some whiskey, girlie?" A man staggered toward her. Della coughed at the foul odor coming from his mouth. She shook her head.

"Do you know where I can find Jim Bridger, or Thomas Fitzpatrick? I heard he's been shot."

The trapper laughed. "Fitzpatrick's been shot alright." He swayed on his feet, and lifted his water bladder to his mouth. The strong odor of whiskey drifted to her nose.

"Where is he?" she demanded.

The trapper spun around, and nearly fell over. He pointed to one of the tents. "Over in yonder tent."

Della skirted around him. She coughed, and inhaled a fresh breath to get the nasty smell out of her nose. A familiar figure rounded the corner of the tent just then, wiping his hands on a piece of cloth. Della's heart skipped a beat.

"Matthew," Della called, and ran toward him.

Matthew's head snapped toward her, a stunned expression on his face. She didn't stop, and threw herself at him, wrapping her arms around his neck.

"I love you," she cried against his neck.

Matthew's arms clamped around her instantly, pushing any remaining air from her lungs. His tight grip lifted her off the ground, and she wrapped her arms more fully around his neck. In the next instant, he set her on her feet, and clasped her face between his hands. His mouth came down on hers like a man deprived of what he needed most.

Della's pulse raced, and her limbs weakened at the urgency in his kiss. She gripped tightly to his shoulders, and parted her lips to his heated kiss. His mouth left hers just as she fought for a breath of air. His lips slid along her cheek, to the side of her neck beneath her ear, and a shiver raced down her spine. Matthew panted for air, burying his face in her hair.

"I love you, Addy. I wasn't gonna let you leave."

He wrapped her in his arms, his muscles tense and trembling, and lifted her to him again.

"Go'n find yerself a tent, why don't ya," someone shouted gruffly, and men's laughter surrounded them.

Matthew eased his hold on her, but didn't set her down. His head drew back, and he smiled. Della's eyes connected with the dark intensity of his stare.

"I'm following my heart," she whispered.

"And I'm holding mine right here in my arms," he said huskily. "I've been a fool for not telling you."

Della reached her hand up. She hesitated for only a second, then touched her palm to the side of Matthew's whiskered cheek. "Does that mean you're now willing to show me the wonders of where you were born and raised?" The corners of her lips twitched with a smile. Happiness and giddiness unlike anything she'd ever felt exploded in her. Matthew loved her. She was free to love him.

Matthew's eyes roamed over her face, and he grinned slowly. He brought one hand behind her head, stroking her hair. "I knew you had an ulterior reason for telling me you love me. You just want to see the Yellowstone. That's been your plan all along, hasn't it?"

He brought her head toward him, and kissed her again. Della pressed her lips to his. Matthew's hold on her tightened, igniting her heart to pound against his chest.

"Ya gonna swallow that girl whole if ya don't ease up."

Della pulled back. Her face flamed at Jim Bridger's words. The trapper cackled loudly. Matthew's eyes didn't leave hers. The intensity of his stare, of the love burning in his eyes, left her breathless. Had it always been there, and she'd simply been afraid to see it for what it was?

"I want to take you home with me as my wife," he rasped. "Say you'll marry me, Addy, and I'll show you all the wonders the Yellowstone has to offer."

The sensation of warm liquid rushing through her body from head to toe left her tingling all over. Tears welled up in her eyes, and a huge lump formed in her throat.

"I want to be your wife," she croaked.

Matthew kissed her again, slow and gentle this time, and set her on her feet. "What's your father going to do to me if I ask him to marry us?" His lips curved upward and his eyes shone with laughter.

Della cocked her head. Her forehead scrunched, and she pursed her lips. Then she burst into laughter. "I think he will say you have his blessing."

She stood on her toes and pressed her lips to the man she loved, and kissed away the astonished look on his face.

CHAPTER THIRTEEN

"What did you mean when you told my father that you'd be sure to keep me in line?"

Della raised her brows, and admired Matthew's broad back. The question had nagged at her all day. He'd never ordered her around before, and that was exactly what his words implied. Would their friendship be different, now that they were married? She'd kept quiet about the subject for hours, but now that they'd stopped for the night, it was at the forefront of her thoughts.

The change in attitude from her father had been nothing short of miraculous. Just as she'd told Matthew, her father had given his blessing to their union, and had officiated over their quick wedding. He'd been truly remorseful for his treatment of her. It had taken her anger to finally make him realize what he'd been doing to her – treating her exactly as he'd treated his wife, trying to force her to his will and thinking it would bring them closer.

After a round of congratulations from some of the trappers who'd come to witness their union, and a tearful good-bye with her father and sister, Matthew had bartered for supplies to get them the last leg of the journey to his family's home. Thomas Fitzpatrick had given Matthew a rifle in appreciation for removing a bullet from his chest, and for saving his life.

"You'll see your father and sister again next spring when we head east," Matthew had told her, holding her in his arms while she stood and watched the wagons disappear from the valley. "We'll go to New York before we head to Boston. Who knows, maybe I'll rethink my original plan, and set up my medical practice in New York instead."

"You'd do that?" She'd glanced up at Matthew in astonishment.

"I don't see what difference it would make where I practice medicine," he'd said with a shrug and a smile.

They'd left the rendezvous shortly after.

"It's still early in the day. I'd like to put a few miles behind us, rather than spending the night here at rendezvous. It's still a long ways to the Yellowstone."

"I know you're anxious to get home," she'd said.

Matthew had held her with one arm around her waist. Love had shone in his eyes when he'd said, "I'm anxious to introduce my bride to my folks."

A loon called to its mate on the tranquil pond where they'd decided to stop for the night. The fluttering of wings broke through the sounds of crickets and frogs, as two ducks took to flight from the water.

Matthew glanced over his shoulder from where he stood by his horse, unloading the pack of blankets and provisions he'd brought from rendezvous. The animal's tail swished lazily at the evening bugs in the air, its head submersed in the tall grasses growing by the water. The horse next to it did the same.

He turned back to what he was doing without answering her question. Della's eyes lingered on her husband's back and shoulders as he lifted the heavy packs to the ground. *Her husband!* If someone had told her this morning that by the evening she would be married, she would have laughed in disbelief.

Matthew dropped the packs, and straightened. He turned, and headed for her, a smug grin on his face. Without warning, he snaked his arm around her waist and pulled her up against him. Della's hands shot up to brace against his shoulders. Heat rushed instantly from her chest to her extremities.

"Your father did say you had to obey me as part of your vows," he said in a sultry tone. He looked down at her, the colors of the evening sun reflected in his dark eyes. "I was only reinforcing his words by saying I'd keep you in line. You're quite a handful, from everything I've seen so far. Your father knows it, so I wanted to reassure him that I was man enough to make you toe the line."

Della eyed the slight upward curve of his lips. His eyes sparkled with amusement. He even winked at her.

"What if I refuse to toe the line?" she challenged.

They'd bantered before, but she'd been reserved then, still unsure of how to act around him. Now that she'd admitted her feelings, and he'd told her he loved her, it came almost naturally.

She'd vowed silently that she'd be a good wife to him. She was used to cooking, washing, keeping a clean house, and most other domestic duties. With marriage came other duties, however, and Della's mouth suddenly went dry at the thought. She had only vague notions of what it meant to lie with a man. In her father's church, the men sat on one side of the aisle, and the women and children on the other, and he'd often preached about the sins of the flesh.

Matthew's arms tightened around her waist, drawing her closer. Sudden dread enveloped her. His roguish grin sent flutters to her stomach. Would he expect her to lie with him tonight?

"I think I can be pretty persuasive to make you do what I want," he said in a low tone, and his mouth came down on hers.

He held her in such a way that her body molded to his while he kissed her. Della's limbs melted in his embrace. She'd never tire of Matthew's kisses, and if that's what he'd do to punish her, she'd be sure to step out of line as often as possible.

"We'd better get camp set up," he breathed against her neck, sending shivers down her spine. "I hope you won't make me sleep on the other side of the fire tonight."

Della stiffened. There it was. He'd be expecting his rights as her husband, and she didn't know what to do. Matthew loosened his hold on her. His forehead furrowed as his eyes traveled over her face. Della held her breath while he scrutinized her, as if he were searching for entry into her mind.

"You're my wife, Addy. There's nothing to be afraid of," he said in that slow, quiet and deep voice that usually soothed away her fears. Not this time.

She nodded, despite her apprehension, unable to form any words. Matthew's fingers grazed her cheek, and he brushed his lips up against hers. His other hand slid slowly from her waist upward, until he touched the underside of her breast through the fabric of her dress.

Della sucked in a quick breath, and closed her eyes, as new sensations raced through her at his simple touch. She leaned into his hand, and he continued to move upward until his palm completely covered her breast. Her knees weakened, and she grasped his arms to steady herself. Her father's preaching all these years about sins of the flesh pounded in her head. His voice grew in intensity, and she fought to shut the noise out. Nothing about this felt wrong, or bad.

The earsplitting sound of twigs breaking and branches snapping broke through the tranquil stillness of early evening. Della jumped away from Matthew, who grabbed her arm, and shoved her to the side. His loud curse drowned out her surprised squeal.

"Get behind that tree, Addy," he commanded loudly.

Her head whipped around. What was happening? Their horses, which had been grazing peacefully by the trees near the pond, spooked. She stumbled as one of the animals darted past her, and ran in the direction from which they had come earlier. Matthew's hand was on her lower back, pushing her forward until she darted behind the trees.

"What's happening?" she panted.

"Run, and climb up that tree," someone yelled. Was that a child's voice? "It's gonna kill you."

"What the hell?" Matthew lunged for the flintlock he'd dropped to the ground with the rest of their belongings, just as a young boy ran past them, heading for one of the trees.

Faster than Della could blink, the boy reached for the

nearest branch, and pulled himself up, and kept climbing. Not a second later, a large monster of an animal appeared through the tall reeds where the boy had been seconds ago. The creature slowed, then trotted past them. It stopped, and turned half way in apparent confusion.

"Don't move," Matthew whispered, holding tight to Della's arm.

He tugged her more firmly behind the trunk of the tree, out of sight of the giant beast. Several branches cracked in the tree next to them. Della caught a glimpse of the child climbing even higher. The giant moose flared its nostrils, then trotted off along the edge of the pond until it disappeared through the tall vegetation. A small flock of birds took to the air, the only indication where the beast had gone.

Matthew released his hold on her, and Addy breathed a sigh of relief. Above them in the tree, the boy laughed.

"I knew I could do it," he yelled triumphantly.

"Lucas, where are you?" Another high-pitched voice called from where the boy and the moose had appeared moments ago.

"I won," the boy in the tree called. "I won the bet." He began to climb down, jumping to the ground from a distance that was more than twice as tall as he.

Matthew lunged forward and grabbed the boy by the arm. "Are you all right?" he asked.

The dark-haired boy grinned broadly, rather than looking afraid or shaken up by his ordeal. Della stared at him. He could have been killed mere seconds ago.

Another boy, older by several years, appeared through the vegetation. He looked around frantically, his chest heaving as if he'd been running for a while.

"You owe me the knife you traded for at rendezvous the other day, Joseph," the smaller boy said, rushing up to the older one.

Matthew stepped forward. He looked from one boy to the other, and his eyes narrowed. "Joseph? Alex Walker's boy?"

"Yessir," the youth nodded. "And that's my brother, Lucas." He leaned forward, and glared at the younger boy. "My stupid brother, Lucas."

"I ain't stupid. I won the bet," the other boy yelled, and lunged at his brother.

"What bet," Matthew asked, his tone low, almost threatening. He grabbed for the boy's arm and held him back from attacking his brother.

Della stepped up beside him. It was written all over Matthew's face that he was getting angry. She put her hand on his arm. He shot her a hasty look before giving his attention to the boys again.

"I told Joseph that I could outrun a moose, and he didn't believe me. So we made a bet. He dared me to try. When we saw that bull on the other side of the pond, I shot at him with my slingshot, so he'd chase me." The boy glared triumphantly at his brother. "And I won."

"I didn't think you'd actually do it," Joseph grumbled.

"Where's your father?" Matthew asked in a low tone.

Della smiled. Judging by the look on Matthew's face, he was ready to lay the boys over his knee.

"Our ma and pa are camped about a mile away on the other side of the pond. We're heading home from the trapper rendezvous," Joseph said, pointing in the direction from which they'd come. He shot an accusing look at his brother. "We were supposed to hunt rabbit."

Matthew frowned. "You could have been killed, you know that," he said to the smaller boy. "A moose is more dangerous than a grizzly. You're lucky you climbed that tree, and that moose was confused by the horses, so it didn't stick around. You put everyone's life in danger."

"He never does what he's told," Joseph said. "Our ma is always saying he's going to put her in an early grave."

"Well, I know your ma and pa, and it's been a few years since I've seen them. You two are probably too young to remember me."

"'Course we remember you," Lucas Walker said cheerfully. "You're Zach Osborne. We just saw you a while ago at rendezvous."

"Zach's my brother," Matthew said. Judging by his voice, his anger had lessened. "I think right now, we need to get you two back to your folks."

"We can find our own way back," Lucas said, a note of pride in his voice. He looked up at Matthew, and studied him suspiciously.

Della held her hand to her mouth to suppress her smile. She didn't doubt the truth of what the little boy's brother had said, that their mother felt her young son would put her in an early grave with worry. He appeared to be quite the handful.

Hooves trampled through the grasses, and Matthew tensed. He held up his rifle, and moved in front of her and the boys. A dark-haired man appeared, leading both their escaped horses.

"Papa caught your horses," Lucas Walker said smugly.

Matthew relaxed, and stepped forward, holding out his hand. The other man clasped it firmly in his.

"Alex, what a surprise to see you."

Alex Walker smiled, and nodded. "Osborne. What are you doing here? I thought you were in a hurry to get . . ." His eyes narrowed, and he leaned slightly forward. "Matthew?" His voice gave away his astonishment. "Evie and I were told just a week ago that you were dead."

Matthew chuckled. "I need to remedy that false rumor. Zach thought I'd been killed, but I'm very much alive."

"So I see."

The man's eyes looked to his sons. He handed the reins to the horses to the older boy, then he looked at Della. Matthew turned, and held out his hand to her, beckoning her to come to his side.

"My wife, Addy," he said, his voice filled with pride. "We were married this morning, just before leaving rendezvous." Turning his head to her, he said, "This is a good friend of the family, Alex Walker."

The older man quickly hid the surprise on his face, and shook her hand. He smiled. "My wife, Evie, is waiting for me and the boys back at our camp." His eyes shot from her to Matthew. "I'm sure she'd be glad for the company, if you'd like to join us since we're heading the same way. We could travel together, at least until the Jackson Valley."

Della's eyes widened in surprise. Having a woman to talk to was most appealing. She glanced up at Matthew. Would he agree to go with this man and his sons to their camp?

"On second thought," Alex said before Matthew could answer. His lips twitched in amusement. "You've already got your camp here. Why don't we meet up tomorrow morning?"

"I think that would be a good idea," Matthew said quickly. He looked at her. "Is that all right with you?"

Della cleared her throat. The fact that he'd asked for her approval melted her heart. "I think that would be fine," she answered. Matthew gave her hand a squeeze.

"We'll see you tomorrow, then." Alex Walker smiled smugly. "Let's go, boys. We're going to have some words when we get back to camp."

Joseph shot a satisfied look at his younger brother, who made a face at him, then ran off ahead of them.

Matthew chuckled. He waited until father and sons were out of sight, then turned to face her. Della looked up at him, the tenderness in his eyes drawing her in.

"Where were we before we got interrupted?" he murmured, and pulled her into his arms.

CHAPTER FOURTEEN

Matthew led the horses back to their grazing spot near the pond, and hobbled their front legs. Releasing Addy out of his arms to tend to their camp had been one of the hardest things he'd ever done. He grinned. His back was turned to his wife, and he ran a hand through his hair. A ripple of heat flowed through him. Addy behaved like two women bundled up in one desirable package. She was daring and courageous in everything she did, and tackled the world head-on, but when it came to intimacy, she was scared to death and innocent.

He cursed her rigid upbringing, and reminded himself for the hundredth time that he had to go slow and show her that love between a man and woman wasn't something to shun or be afraid of.

Addy spread out the blankets on the ground while he gathered wood and started a fire. Matthew glanced at the clear sky. The sun had already sunk deep into the horizon, and stars were starting to appear in the twilight sky. The chorus of frogs grew louder around them. She unpacked some biscuits and jerky from their provisions, and handed him the food.

"That boy was a handful," Addy said, after she'd eaten in silence. She sat on the furs beside him, wringing her hands in her lap, staring toward the water.

Matthew swallowed his last bite of biscuit, and washed it down with a drink from his water skin. He offered it to her, along with a reassuring smile. Would they be sharing a quiet meal at this very moment if the Walker boys and their dangerous escapades hadn't interrupted them?

Matthew tugged on her hand and pulled her closer. He grinned. "Maybe we'll have one just like him."

"If we do, I doubt he'd be provoking a moose, and chasing it through New York," Addy retorted with a smile.

"There are moose in New York, too." Matthew's grin widened. His arm wrapped around her waist, and he drew her more fully against his side.

"Not in the city." Addy stiffened slightly, but quickly relaxed against him.

It was all the encouragement he needed. Matthew leaned toward her. His lips grazed the side of her soft cheek. She shuddered in his arm when he kissed her just below her ear. Heat pooled in his gut at her reaction.

"I think you'll be a wonderful mother someday," he murmured.

He reached his hand up to cup her cheek, and turned her face to his. Her eyes glowed with desire when she looked at him, even if she didn't realize it.

"Don't hide under those blankets tonight." He lightly touched his lips to hers.

Addy nodded, her eyes wide. Matthew wrapped his

arms more fully around her, and pulled her onto his lap. She sucked in an audible breath. He slid his hand behind her neck, and pulled her to him. Her willing response when he kissed her sent renewed waves of desire crashing through him.

"I love you, Addy. You're the most wonderful woman I've ever met. There's no shame when a husband loves his wife."

"Show me," she whispered, and brought her hand up to his cheek, drawing him closer.

Matthew groaned at her response. His hands traveled up and down her back, caressing the contours of her spine, then along her hips, until her body softened to his touch, and she was no longer tense. He kissed her lips, her cheeks, and down her neck, struggling for a breath of air. When she pressed her body to his, her own breathing becoming more ragged, his heart raced out of control.

He stopped touching her long enough to pull his shirt up and over his head, then wrapped his arms more fully around hers and kissed her again. Slowly, her fingers explored along the planes of his back, along his shoulders, and down his chest. Matthew leaned back against the furs, pulling her with him, then rolled her onto her back.

Touching her with clothes between them was no longer enough. He unbuttoned her dress while murmuring in her ear that he loved her. Addy wriggled beneath him, bringing her hands between them to help him with the buttons. She shivered in his arms when he undressed her fully. Matthew stared down at her, tugging on the strings of her chemise, until the final layer of her clothes fell away. His eyes roamed her face before he took in the rest of her.

The deep purple and red hues shimmering on the horizon as the sun disappeared to give way to night reflected in the warm glow in Addy's eyes. The complete look of trust on her face as she looked up at him, sent a surge of love through him with a force so strong it almost hurt.

"You're beautiful," he whispered.

She smiled tentatively, and reached for him. Matthew covered her with his body, and gathered her to him. The feel of her skin against his seared him like hot embers.

"My father is wrong," she murmured against his neck. Her words sent another wave of pleasure through him. The light strokes of her fingers along his back as she explored him nearly drove him mad.

"Your father is the last person I want to talk about right now," he growled. "I'm going to make you forget everything he's told you about how it should be between a man and woman."

"You've already done that", she whispered, and dug her fingers into his back.

Matthew covered her mouth with his. Addy writhed beneath him when he nuzzled her ear, then grazed his lips down her neck and to her breasts. His hands stroked along the soft curves of her hips and thighs, then back up to explore the rest of her. Her breathing quickened, and her own exploring hands raked more urgently down his back.

"I love you, Matthew," she mumbled in a breathless voice.

Matthew kissed her again, unhurriedly. He wasn't going to rush this, giving her time to explore and touch, and get to know him, just as he wanted to get to know her.

She hesitated slightly when he guided her hand to the ties that held his britches to his hips. His gut clenched when she helped him push the britches down his legs without further reservation.

"Come here," he rasped, gathering her back into his arms. "I want to feel you."

She pressed against him, raising her leg and rubbing her foot against the outside of his thigh. Matthew stroked her hips and the dip in her waist until her breathing became ragged. He kissed her long and slow until she squirmed beneath him.

"I like having you touch me," she whispered, and gripped his shoulders. "And I like touching you."

Matthew groaned. His stomach tightened almost painfully, and heat seared through him. He couldn't wait any longer. He gathered her to him and eased her legs apart. Settling between her thighs, he took her innocence with one swift stroke. Just as she inhaled sharply, he covered her mouth with his, and waited until she relaxed against him. Her soft gasps and moans when he moved inside her filled his heart to near bursting. He grasped her around the waist, and rolled onto his back, bringing her fully on top of him to give her complete control to take them both to heaven and back.

Della lay on her side, bracing her upper body on her elbow. Her hair spilled down the sides of her face, tickling her bare arms. She smiled, and lightly touched her fingers to Matthew's chest. His warm skin sent ripples up her arms, and she followed the contours of his muscles up his shoulders and back down to his abdomen.

His slow, even breathing from a second ago became erratic. Before she could blink, a hand snaked up and grasped her around her wrist. Della squealed and laughed, and before she had the chance to pull back, he was on top of her. Matthew braced his weight on one elbow and stared down at her, his dark eyes and roguish grin sending rippled of delight through her.

"I've created an insatiable hellion," he growled, and kissed her with such tender passion, all air left her lungs.

He pulled the buffalo robe fully over their heads, and made love to her until they both lay panting in each other's arms.

"You're going to be the death of me. I may not make it home alive after all," he grumbled, a satisfied smile on his face.

"I don't think you've reached the end of your stamina yet. I have complete faith that you'll be alive and well by the time we see your family."

Matthew leaned down and kissed her again. "I'm going to be the happiest man alive by the time we get to the Madison Valley, although my father and brother-in-law will challenge that claim."

"You think we'll be home with them by the end of today?" Della wound her arms around his neck.

"Not if you keep me occupied under this buffalo hide all morning."

"I don't mind if it takes another day," she purred, and smiled coyly up at him.

Matthew rolled to his back. He gathered her in his

arms, and held her against him. Love flowed through her like the heat from the hot springs she'd seen yesterday. Today, she'd be married for two weeks, and with each day she loved her husband more. His heart beat strong against her palm that she held to his chest.

She smiled. How could anyone think that the love shared between a husband and wife was anything but beautiful and enjoyable? He was right that she was insatiable. She would never stop loving him. Her wedding night had been frightening and wondrous at the same time. Matthew's lovemaking was both strong and tender, and she delighted in his touch.

When they'd broken camp the morning after their wedding night, she'd almost regretted agreeing to accompany the Walkers for part of the way through the mountains. Evie Walker, however, had become a wonderful friend. The love between her and her husband was clear to see, and while she had her hands full with her two sons, her husband doted on her.

They'd parted ways when they'd reached a valley that stretched along the base of one of the most magnificent mountain ranges she had ever seen. The snow-capped peaks of the Teewinots, Matthew's name for the towering mountains ahead, were visible for miles as they rose into the sky. They'd followed the course of a winding river aptly named the Snake, and Evie had told them to send her regards to Matthew's parents when they parted ways.

That had been a week ago. Matthew had led her through dense forests, over high mountains, and along fast-flowing rivers, until they came to the largest lake she'd ever seen. Waves crashed along its shores as if she was standing by the ocean. Off in the distance, more snow-capped mountains lined the horizon, and the forest continued for as far as the eye could see.

Della's eyes had widened with wonder when she saw her first pools of hot water. The brilliant blue and orange colors beckoned to her, and she'd never seen such pristine clear water before. Matthew had held her back, cautioning her from getting too close.

"They're beautiful, but also deadly," he'd said. "No one survives if they fall into one of these."

She'd watched in amusement as hot mud bubbled like thick porridge in a kettle over the fire, sometimes splattering her dress. She'd stepped back quickly when a splash of mud touched her skin. Matthew had laughed.

"I told you it's hot, but I guess you had to find out for yourself."

"What is that over there?" She'd pointed toward the lake, where steam rose along the water's edge.

"There are hot springs even under the water all along this lakeshore. My guess is, you'd find them further out in the lake as well, but the water is so cold, you'd die if you stayed in it too long trying to investigate."

Della shook her head in amazement. "I'll burn to death over here." She'd pointed to a hot spring not far from shore. "And die of exposure over there."

"Something like that," Matthew had said, and led her away from the area once she'd seen enough.

"What other wonders are there to see?" she'd asked eagerly.

"We'll have all summer to explore, and even this winter if we don't get snowed in," he'd whispered against her neck. "And even that won't be enough time to see it all."

"Then we'll have to return to visit your family as often as possible," she'd replied with a sly smile.

Matthew had led her away from the lake, and back to where they'd set up camp, apparently eager to put an end to that day's sightseeing. By the time he'd carried her to their blankets, she'd had no objections.

CHAPTER FIFTEEN

Matthew tensed next to her under the buffalo robe. His hand slid slowly upward and out from under the covering where he kept his belt and weapons. Della stared at him in the dim light under the covers. He didn't make a sound. She'd learned by now that he didn't react like this for no reason. Something had alerted him. Quietly, he moved away from her and out from under the robe, apparently unconcerned about his complete nudity.

Twigs snapped somewhere close by, and a dog barked.

"Come here, Grizzly," Matthew said loudly.

Della kept a tight hold on her covers. She poked her head out just enough to see. Matthew slipped into his britches at that moment, and a large dog, or was it a wolf, danced happily around his feet.

"Well look what the sky people dropped on the ground. I don't believe it. Matthew?"

A man's loud voice drew closer. He laughed, sounding both happy and in disbelief. Della's heart sped up in horror. She was under the robe, completely nude, and her dress was too far away to reach. She snatched the covers back over her head.

"Chase," Matthew said in greeting. "What are you doing this far south?"

Rather than answer, the other man said, "Well, I've been wanting to head up a search for you since Zach came home about a week ago to tell us you were dead," he said slowly. "I told him I was heading toward the Tetons, and from there, to the Wind River. Zach, Sam and Touch the Cloud were going to catch up in a few days."

"Well, you can save yourself the trouble. I'm alive and well."

"Yeah, you are." The other man laughed. "I can already hear Elk Runner saying that the sky people must have great plans for you if they brought you back from the dead."

Della lowered the robe again out of curiosity, just enough to see. A tall, blond woodsman stood a short distance away. His eyes fell on the robes just then. His brows rose, and a wide grin spread across his face. To Della's mortification, he looked directly at her, and nudged his chin in her direction.

"And that's the way I'd wanna die, too. Good for you, man."

Matthew frowned, and stepped in front of the robes, obstructing the tall man's view.

"Are you on foot?" he asked gruffly.

"Left my horse back a ways. Grizzly sniffed you out, and I thought I'd better come and check it out."

"If you wouldn't mind, go back to your horse, and we'll catch up with you."

Laughter rumbled from the other man. "Sure thing. It's good to have you home, Matt." He slapped Matthew on the back, and clasped his arm before he turned and whistled. The dog followed on his heels, and the two disappeared into the trees.

Della breathed a sigh of relief. She raised herself to a sitting position, firmly holding the robe against her chest. Matthew knelt beside her, and touched his hand to the top of her head, stroking it slowly down the length of her hair.

"That was my brother-in-law, Chase Russell," he said, an apologetic look on his face. "I'll introduce you later."

He handed her clothing to her, and Della quickly dressed while Matthew broke camp. Mounting their horses, it didn't take long to find the spot where the woodsman waited with his dog along the banks of the river.

"Chase, I'd like you to meet my wife, Addy," Matthew said when they came up alongside his brother-in-law.

Chase's easy grin enhanced his handsome features, and Della had no doubt that he knew it. He reached for her hand, and clasped it firmly in his.

"How'd you snag this guy?" he asked, nodding toward Matthew.

Della's forehead scrunched in confusion. She'd had trouble understanding some of the mountain men at rendezvous, and this man's words were just as strange, but in a different way.

His eyes widened suddenly, and he snapped his fingers, then he pointed from Matthew to her. "You're the girl Matthew went to rescue from a band of Pawnee, when he got shot by an arrow. Zach told us." He laughed. "Guess he left out the rest of the story."

"I'm eager to get home and hear how Zach managed to get away from the Pawnee, too," Matthew said.

He nudged his horse, and Della followed as he led the way along the banks of the river. Chase kept up a lively conversation, filling Matthew in on his parents' reaction to news of his death, about his wife and daughters, and general news of people they both knew. Della soon tuned him out since she didn't know anything about what was being said.

She lost herself in the beauty of her surroundings instead. She marveled at the steaming water that ran into the river in areas, and the brilliant orange and green colors that lined these rivulets and run-offs. The men soon left the river, and followed narrow deer trails through a thickly wooded forest. Many times, the horses had to navigate over or around fallen trees that lay around in abundance.

By mid-afternoon, the forest opened into a lush green meadow, and a wide stream meandered through it. They guided their horses through the water to the opposite bank. The dog barked happily, and ran ahead of them. Della looked into the distance. Thin wisps of smoke rose into the air, and two cabins came into view. It appeared as if the stream met up with another river, and formed a wider body of water that continued to flow through the valley.

Matthew pulled his horse up alongside hers. He smiled broadly, and pointed toward the cabins, which were nestled along a hillside blanketed in pine trees.

"We're home," he said, and reached for her hand.

Della's eyes roamed over the scenery. A steep mountain rose out of the valley on the left. The river created a wide arc and flowed westward, and the cabins stood to the right, overlooking the river. They'd have a direct view of the steep mountain.

"It's beautiful," she whispered, taking it all in.

"Happy homecoming," Chase called loudly, and rode ahead of them. "I'll let you tell the folks that you're here."

Chase stopped in front of one of the cabins, while Matthew guided his horse to the other. A dark-haired woman wearing britches rushed to greet Chase, then she ran toward Matthew, calling his name repeatedly. He dismounted and opened his arms.

"We thought you were dead," She sobbed against him.

Matthew held her tight, then peeled her arms away from him. "We'll tell you the story when we're all together," he said. "Sarah, meet my wife, Addy."

Matthew helped Della from her horse. His sister, Sarah, pulled her into a firm embrace. "You don't know how happy I am," she cried.

"I'm sure Matthew's homecoming must be such a relief to your heavy heart," Della said quietly, when she pulled out of her sister-in-law's embrace. She would have recognized her anywhere. Matthew had told her all about his only sister, and how she'd grown up always trying to best her brothers, and usually succeeded.

"Matthew? Oh my God. Matthew?"

The door to the other cabin ripped open, and a short woman with blond hair rushed out. She threw herself into Matthew's arms just as Sarah had done, and cried loudly.

Matthew embraced his mother, who clung to him as if she'd never let him go. She was a petite woman, and

Matthew lifted her easily off the ground. They stood and hugged for minutes. Della wiped at the tears in her eyes, and Sarah sniffled next to her, gripping her hand.

"Chase rode off to find Papa, Zach, and Sam," Sarah said. "They went hunting to have meat for when they set out to look for you."

"Mama, I'd like you to meet someone," Matthew said, still holding his mother in his arms.

Aimee Osborne loosened her hold on her son, but not completely. She raised her head to look up at him, and clasped her palm against his cheek.

"When Zach told us you were dead, I . . . " she whispered. Fresh tears rolled down her face, and she smiled.

"It's all right, Mama. Zach didn't know. He did the right thing by coming home rather than staying in hostile Indian territory."

Matthew looked toward Della. He grinned. "Mama, come and meet my wife."

Mrs. Osborne covered the surprised look on her face fairly quickly. Della held her breath when their eyes met. This was Matthew's mother. Would she welcome her?

The petite woman pulled away from her son. Her eyes widened in astonishment. She glanced toward Matthew.

"Today is just full of happy surprises," she said, then held out her arms.

Della hesitated. Before she could move, Matthew's mother walked up to her and pulled her into a warm hug. Della's heart melted. She wrapped her arms around the older woman's back. The sensation of warmth filled her, as if this woman's love was pouring straight from her into Della.

"This is Adelle, Mama. I call her Addy. She saved my life."

Mrs. Osborne's arms around her tightened, the strength in her grip belying her small stature.

"It's so good to have you in the family, Addy," she whispered. "Any woman my son thinks of highly enough to marry must be someone very special."

"I'm happy to be part of the family, Mrs. Osborne," Della croaked. Her throat constricted as she held back her tears.

"It's Aimee, or . . . you can call me Mama."

Della blinked, and looked into the woman's soft blue eyes, which reflected love and joy. She wasn't so petite, after all. Or perhaps, Della was just as small, since they seemed to be about the same height.

"Let's go inside," Aimee said brightly. She reached for Della's hand, and also for Matthew's. "We'll wait for your father and brothers, and then you two have to tell us everything that's happened. In the meantime, you've got to be hungry and thirsty."

Della met Matthew's glance and smile, and followed him and his mother into the cabin. She sat at the table while Aimee insisted on fixing them something to eat. Matthew pulled Della onto his lap, and kissed the back of her neck. Della's face flamed when Aimee turned from working at the bench along one wall of the large room. She smiled brightly. Matthew's display of affection didn't seem to bother her, and Della relaxed.

The door burst open, and Chase walked in, carrying a little girl, followed by Sarah, who carried an even younger child in her arms. Three other men followed closely on their heels. Della stiffened, and slid from Matthew's lap. He stood, and held out his hand.

An older man, with the same physique as Matthew, but black, shoulder-length hair, pulled him into his embrace, then slapped his back. Matthew clasped his father's arm when they separated.

The ritual repeated twice more, first with Zach, then with a younger man, who had to be Matthew's brother, Samuel. Aimee walked up to them, and Matthew's father instantly wrapped his arm around her waist and pulled her close. The two exchanged a quick look that left Della staring. There was an unmistakable spark of love in that brief exchange.

After more tearful introductions and everyone welcoming her into the family, they all settled around the table in the center of the room. Matthew told the story of how Della had found him, their escape from the Pawnee, and their journey here.

"Didn't I tell you I'd find him and bring him home?" Chase looked at Zach, then winked at Matthew.

"I searched for you. I thought those Injuns took your body. I followed the river to see if you'd been swept downstream. Had I known you were alive . . ." Zach broke off and shook his head.

Matthew chuckled. "You were never the best tracker in the family. No wonder Sarah always outsmarted you." He glanced around the room. "We backtracked, and stayed out of sight for a few days while Addy tended to me. We headed south before going north again, once we were out of Pawnee territory."

Daniel Osborne sat quietly, his wife on his lap. She leaned her head on his broad shoulder, a content smile on her face. The dark lines under her eyes were testament to her anguish since receiving the news that her son was dead, and she'd most likely endured a week of sleepless nights. She could rest peacefully tonight.

Della leaned against Matthew, who'd wrapped one arm around her waist and held her to him on his lap. She listened while he told his story, her eyes moving discreetly from Daniel to Aimee. Matthew shared characteristics with both his parents. While he had his mother's quick smile and light hair, his features resembled his father, and so did his self-assured, quiet mannerisms.

Much later, when she lay in her husband's arms and everyone else had gone to bed, Della smiled up at Matthew in the darkness. He held her close, and she rested her head against his chest, listening to the strong, steady beating of his heart.

"Your family is wonderful, and this place is spectacular beyond words," she whispered.

Matthew's arms tightened around her. "I hope you'll be content to be a lowly doctor's wife when we head back east in the spring."

Della kissed his arm. "I don't care where home is, as long as it's with you."

Matthew rolled her onto her back. "Wherever we are, I know you and I are going to do great things together." He leaned over her, and kissed her long and slow. "But right now, I'm going to enjoy this Yellowstone homecoming."

DEAR READER

When a reader approached me with the request for Matthew Osborne's story, I knew instantly what the basic plot for his book would be. Way back in 2012, when I was deep in research for a different book set along the Oregon Trail (Come Home to Me), I came across a true story about a father of an emigrant family who, half-jokingly, gave one of his daughters in trade to a Native American the wagon train encountered along the way. He never thought the Indian would hold him to his word.

The story stuck with me, and I had intended to use it for the second book in the Teton Romance Trilogy when I was plotting that series. Well, it never made it into any of the Teton books (I couldn't resist to bring the Walker boys from the Teton stories into this book for a cameo). In the back of my mind, I always wanted the Osborne brothers to perhaps scout for a wagon train, but the time period just didn't fit.

Emigrants didn't start moving west in wagon trains

until 1843, with the height of migration in the early 1850's. There were, however, groups of missionaries who traveled west. In 1836, Marcus and Narcissa Whitman, along with a few other missionary couples, were the first to head west for Oregon, led by fur trappers Milton Sublette and Thomas Fitzpatrick.

Jim Bridger was a famous trapper, mountain man, scout, and explorer. He was one of the first white men to see the geysers of Yellowstone. Because of his reputation as a "teller of tall tales", no one in the east believed his stories of what he'd seen. His tales as written in this story are taken from actual accounts.

Fort Williams was the original name of Fort Laramie. In 1838 when this story takes place, the fort was a trapper outpost, not a military fort. It was founded by fur trapper William Sublette in 1834. The army bought the outpost in 1849 to establish a base to protect the wagon trains on the Oregon Trail.

The fur traders and mountain men held annual rendezvous, or get-togethers to trade and restock on supplies, from 1825 until about 1841. The 1838 rendezvous was held in the Wind River Basin, near the present-day town of Riverton, Wyoming, as described in this story.

Willow bark contains a chemical called salicin, which is similar to aspirin. Its pain relieving properties has been known throughout history. The ancient Greeks chewed on the bark to relieve pain and fever. The Native Americans made tea from the bark for aches and pains, and poultices to help heal abscesses.

Please join my list of awesome readers, and get exclusive content, such as the unpublished Prologue, and first three chapters that were cut from the original manuscript for Yellowstone Heart Song just for signing up! Find out about Aimee's encounter with Zach before she time traveled.

You'll also be kept up-to-date with the characters from the Yellowstone series in my popular exclusive monthly "Aimee's Journal" entries, sneak peeks, free book offers, behind the scenes info, latest releases, and much more!

Go to: http://www.subscribepage.com/j3x0h0 on your web browser to sign up.

Many of my readers have asked for a timeline for both the **Yellowstone series** as well as the **Teton Trilogy** and the **Wilderness Brides Series**, since the three series are related (by setting and time period) and characters from one series make cameo appearances in the other. Please email me, and I will get you a download link.

peggy@peggylhenderson.com

Yellowstone Romance Series:

(in recommended reading order)

Yellowstone Heart Song

Return to Yellowstone

A Yellowstone Christmas

Yellowstone Redemption
Yellowstone Reflections
A Yellowstone Homecoming
Yellowstone Love Notes
A Yellowstone Season of Giving
Yellowstone Awakening
Yellowstone Dawn
Yellowstone Deception
A Yellowstone Promise
Yellowstone Origins
Yellowstone Legacy
Yellowstone Legends

ACKNOWLEDGMENTS

As always, I couldn't do this without my support team: My wonderful editor, Barbara Ouradnik, who not only makes me use proper grammar, but also keeps my characters and plot on track.

Also, my fabulous beta readers on this book, who find the little plot mistakes and pesky typos that are so easy to miss, and give me unbiased feedback: Heather Belleguelle, Lisa Bynum, Sonja Carroll, Shirl Deems, Kathie Hamilton, and Hilarie Smith.

A special thanks to Abby Braga, who campaigned relentlessly for this book to get written. Finally, thank you to a member of the Pioneer Hearts Facebook group who was the winner of a contest to name the heroine in this story.

ABOUT THE AUTHOR

Peggy L Henderson is an award-winning, best-selling western historical and time travel romance author of the Yellowstone Romance Series, Second Chances Time Travel Romance Series, Teton Romance Trilogy, and Wilderness Brides Series. She was also a contributing author in the unprecedented 50-book American Mail Order Brides Series, contributing Book #15, Emma: Bride of Kentucky, the multi-author Timeless Hearts Time Travel Series, and the multi-author Burnt River Contemporary Western Series.

When she's not writing about Yellowstone, the Tetons, or the old west, she's out hiking the trails, spending time with her family and pets, or catching up on much-needed sleep. She is happily married to her high school sweetheart. They live in Yellowstone National Park, where many of her books are set.

Peggy is always happy to hear from her readers!

To get in touch with Peggy:
www.peggylhenderson.com
peggy@peggylhenderson.com

CPSIA information can be obtained
at www.ICGtesting.com
Printed in the USA
BVHW041251100822
644153BV00011B/91

9 781096 694212